THE TALL TEXAN

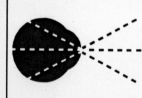

This Large Print Book carries the
Seal of Approval of N.A.V.H.

THE TALL TEXAN

LEE E. WELLS

WHEELER PUBLISHING
A part of Gale, Cengage Learning

GALE
CENGAGE Learning·

Detroit • New York • San Francisco • New Haven, Conn • Waterville, Maine • London

GALE
CENGAGE Learning®

LIBRARY OF CONGRESS CATALOGING-IN-PUBLICATION DATA

Wells, Lee E., 1907-1982.
   The tall Texan / by Lee E. Wells. — Large print ed.
     p. cm. — (Wheeler Publishing large print western)
   ISBN-13: 978-1-4104-4771-5 (pbk.)
   ISBN-10: 1-4104-4771-5 (pbk.)
   1. Large type books. I. Title.
PS3545.E5425T44 2012
813'.54—dc23
                                    2012001790

Published in 2012 by arrangement with Golden West Literary Agency.

Printed in the United States of America
1 2 3 4 5   16 15 14 13 12
FD123

for Helen

I

At long last, to Bob James' relief, the dirt road began to climb low hills lifting out of the Salt River Valley and Phoenix now lay far behind. At the crest of the long, gentle slope, Bob looked back over a wide shoulder, thinking of the town back there and the lanky stranger who had sought him out last night, a man who smiled a lot but whose eyes did not quite hold the warmth of voice and lips. After days of long and steady riding, Bob had come to the saloon following supper at the hotel.

This near to his destination, uncertainty had come alive. Could he do the job? Would the men who counted think they had made a mistake? After two shots of whiskey, he looked at himself in the bar mirror and mentally spoke in defiance to his reflected image.

"They hired you, didn't they? They checked you clean back to where you were born. They know all about you, don't they? So how you figure they made a mistake?"

Just then a voice had lifted back of him, near the batwings. "Is there a gent called Bob James here?"

Long dealing with outlaws and treachery guns checked Bob's instinctive turn. In the bar mirror Bob spotted the man as he took another step into the room and called again.

"Bob James?"

Bob turned but cleared his arm and holster from the bar. "Here! I'm James."

The man had come up, and no one with violence on his mind walked with that ease. A man no more than his own thirty years, Bob judged, who might once have been a drifter but now had a job of sorts — puncher, perhaps. Long nose and mouth, confident outside but wary within, despite the smile.

"Pleased to meet you, Bob James. You're the man who's going to wear the badge in Singara?"

"Who told you that?"

The stranger bellied against the bar. "I reckon everyone in Singara has knowed for weeks now . . . Bartender! Drinks for us! . . . A pleasure, Sheriff."

"Not yet, friend."

The stranger's glance touched on Bob's

8

shirt, devoid of badge. "Will be! Will be! Here's to law in Singara!"

Bob lifted the shotglass in acknowledgment. "Who are you?"

"They call me Sonora. Left Singara yesterday, heading to Florence. They told me you might be here, so figured I'd sort of make you welcome ahead of time."

"Thanks. Who told you?"

"My boss, for one. Maybe a dozen others. Just riding through but I chanced you'd be here. Sure 'nough!"

"Who's your boss?"

"Big man, ain't you? About as big as I've seen."

"Your size, about."

Sonora placed a hand on Bob's arm, eyed the wide shoulders and deep chest, then scratched his head. "I'd not believe it. You just look big. Muscles all filled out. Sure tricks a feller, first look. Hear you come from a hell-shooting town down in New Mexico. Must be handy with a Colt."

"I held a deputy job three years, if that's what you mean."

"Sure do. That's what we need in Singara. You get on up there and take over. I'll see you before long."

He turned and started toward the batwings. Bob called, "Wait a minute! A lot

9

I don't know about you."

"Shucks, ask anyone in Singara about Sonora when you get there. See you soon."

He was gone. Bob stood a moment then strode after him. He stepped out onto the saloon porch and had to adjust his eyes to the night's darkness, broken only by bars of lamplight here and there. Dark figures moved along the board walk and loomed shadowy high on horseback out in the street. Sonora was lost among them.

Bob returned to the bar, caught the eyes of the bartender. "The man who was just with me — who was he?"

"Never saw him before, friend."

"Called himself Sonora — from Singara."

"Never heard of him. But there's lots of folks pass through Phoenix from Singara way."

Bob was just as puzzled this morning as he had been last night. Friendly cuss, Sonora, give him that. Might be just what he said, rider on business for his ranch. Bob touched his impatient horse with his spur. The animal, with a snort of relief, set itself to the road and the ride ahead. Bob pulled his wide hat brim lower over his eyes, dismissing Sonora.

Bob thought the line of barren, low hills through which the road found a way would open on another valley. Instead, there was a shallow swale where the road dipped and lifted to another line of rocky mounds stretching to either side as far as he could see. Then another — and another. A road runner popped from behind an ocotillo clump. The awkward, brown bird, scrawny neck extended, crazy-skittered ahead for many yards and then disappeared.

More hills, row on row of them, until Bob tired of expecting his first sight of Singara. But it could not be far, he knew. The thought made uncertainty flood him again. He took off his hat and passed sleeved arm over his forehead with a nervous gesture.

The town would look him over, make him welcome, shake his hand, buy him drinks and see that he had a place to stay. Friendly — but watchful, judging. He couldn't blame them. They'd hired his gun to back the law badge they'd pin on him and they'd want to know it was right from the minute they first saw him.

Not that he hadn't told them in letters back and forth. Army — last year of the War and then Indian-fighting cavalry for three years more. Freighter and gold rider for a spell. Then deputy sheriff in Balado for six years. No matter how lawless Singara was, it couldn't hold a candle to Balado. That's why they took one of its deputies rather than a sheriff from some more peaceful town.

Bob sighed as another row of monotonous hills came in sight over the crest of the near ones. They'd judge — the way he walked and talked and how he rode and wore his gun. They'd *know* when the first bit of trouble came along, but until then he'd be examined like a strange horse up for sale.

He looked at the sky, judging the time from the sun and estimating the remaining miles to Singara. Not far. As soon as he busted out of these blasted hills, he'd pull in, beat the dust off his clothes and slick his hair. At least he'd look like the lawman they'd hired.

He crested a low ridge and ahead — more hills! He sighed in exasperation as the horse moved down the slope to the bottom of the swale and set itself for the slope ahead. Bob shifted in a sudden, irritable move.

He felt the tug at his shirt and the streak of fire along his back simultaneously with the flat crack of a rifle. He sank spurs and twisted savagely on the reins in a single, instinctive motion. The horse burst down the swale as a second bullet whined close to the left. Bob's Colt flashed into his hand as he twisted about in time to see the thin wisp of smoke from the crest of one of the hummocks.

Bob's glance flashed to either side, and a brutal tug on the reins turned the horse sharply left and up the slope between the same line of rocks behind which the ambusher hid. A third shot whistled just behind Bob as he leaned low in the saddle, raking spurs. Rock walls flashed high to either side and he was momentarily safe from further attack.

He reined in. He dropped Colt into holster and pulled his rifle from its scabbard as he pictured the line of hills that hid both him and the ambusher. In a matter of seconds, long lips angrily set, he spurred his mount along the shallow canyon, down into the swale and up into the protection of the second line of hills, through them and sharply to the left.

He now had two rows of peaked rocks between him and the hidden rifleman. The unknown might still be up there in the rocks, or he might be on horseback now. If so, he could ride in any direction — along the distant swale where Bob had fled, or back this way. Or he might wait to see if his quarry appeared again. If Bob made a wrong guess, the next bushwhack bullet could score.

Bob came to the main road and halted, still in the protection of the hills. He listened as his eyes sought the broken pinnacles. He heard nothing, saw nothing. He set spurs and dashed across the road, disappeared beyond it.

He counted three of the monotonous hillocks and then turned left, paralleling the road back toward Phoenix. He held his rifle ready, shell jacked into the chamber. He eased out into the open, eyes constantly moving, and sought the protection of the next shallow canyon. Reaching it, he swiftly dismounted, ground-tied the horse and scrambled up the near slope. Close to the summit, he dropped to his knees and inched to a point where he could see beyond the crest.

The swale below stood empty and Bob's lips flattened in disappointment. A flick of motion far to his left brought his eyes around, narrowed and sharp. A man on a bay horse moved cautiously out into the swale. Bob dropped flat as the distant rider, rifle held ready, searched slowly along the crests.

Bob grimly and slowly counted twenty before he again edged his head above the rock crown. He felt a surge of grim elation. The rider looked the other way. His wide-brimmed hat hid his face. Not that it mattered. Anyone this far from Balado would be a stranger. Then why the ambush? Robbery?

Bob had no time to decide. The man below threw off tension and shoved his rifle back in the scabbard. He started to turn, but Bob slid below the crest and scrambled down the slope to his horse. He swept up reins and swung into saddle. He held the horse still, bent forward and clamped his hand across its muzzle.

The animal tossed its head but submitted to the indignity. Watching the end of the shallow pass between the hills, Bob waited for so long he began to believe he had misjudged the direction of his quarry. But at that moment horse and rider passed at a fast trot across the far opening and was gone.

Bob spoke softly and moved the horse along the canyon to emerge into the swale beyond. Not far ahead, the ambusher rode unheedingly. Bob set spurs, breaking into a gallop. The echoing thunder of hooves caused the man ahead to throw a startled look back over his shoulder.

Bob shouted in grim anger, "Looking for — ?"

He saw the swift drop of the man's hand

15

to his holster. Bob swerved his mount as his own hand slapped against a walnut Colt handle and the weapon flashed up. Fire winked evilly at him and smoke billowed but the bullet went wide. Bob's Colt bucked back within his fist.

The ambusher jerked as the slug hit him and his hands spasmodically opened. The gun fell in a whirling flash and the reins dropped as the man tumbled back over the cantle and fell just beyond his mount's rump. The animal snorted and kicked, hooves whipping savagely over the slack body. Bob spurred forward to grab the trailing reins and subdue the plunging animal.

He dismounted then and turned to the man who lay on the ground, face down, hat lying off to one side. He was dead. Bob knew from the flaccid body. He turned it over and saw the red-stained shirt.

His eyes widened as he looked at the face and he could not help his exclamation.

"Sonora!"

II

Bob started a search for identification, for some indication of what had sent this stranger on a bushwhack trail. Shirt pockets held only blood-stained tobacco sack and papers, soiled matches. Trouser pockets produced a few coins and a leather pouch that contained crumpled currency. There were no papers to show who Sonora might be. For that matter, Bob thought, even the dead man's statement that he had come from Singara might be a lie.

It took heartfelt cursing at the skittish horses and a great deal of muscle, but finally Bob had Sonora face down across his own saddle, arms and legs dangling. Bob lashed the body in place and then remounted. He rode back down the swale to the road and turned northwest along it, heading for Singara.

Traversing the unending monotony of the hills, he tried to solve the problem of Sonora. It became plain that last night's meeting was not by chance. Sonora had made sure of his quarry and Lord knew how long he had waited in Phoenix to do it. He must have sought in all the saloons and hotels, Bob concluded, and that meant a definite assignment — unless the man sought revenge for some outlaw kin who might have tangled with the law in Balado and lost. Bob sighed in frustration. The man had not come out of the past, but the present — or the immediate future, for someone must not want Bob in Singara.

17

He rode slowly to the ridge of the swale, exactly like hundreds of others behind him. But at the crest he drew rein in pleased surprise. Ahead lay a huge valley, the hills falling away to form an irregular crescent to the north. He saw the distant stores and houses of Singara.

Journey's end, he thought with relief, and then he looked back at the corpse. Who were Sonora's friends in Singara? Considering the ambush, extend the question to who would Bob James' friends be and who his enemies? Bob touched spurs and moved down the slope toward the town.

His uncertainties, submerged for so long, came back full force. What would they think of him up ahead? His lips twisted mirthlessly. Here he rode in with a man killed by his bullet. A hell of a way to take over a new job! He unconsciously straightened as he approached the town's first structure, an adobe hovel. The road made a curve at a point where another road from the north joined it and became the main street of the town.

As he passed the open door of the adobe, a Mexican peered out with faint curiosity that became frozen surprise when he saw the lashed body. The man whipped back inside the hut.

Now Bob could see a part of Singara's main street. Far ahead, it curved again but, within view, stood false front stores and buildings, facing one another across the dusty thoroughfare. Horses stood hip-shot at hitchracks. A loaded buckboard wheeled away around the far curve and disappeared. He saw a few people on the planked walks before the buildings.

Gray eyes searched the structures and signs, sought a name that might have appeared in the letters he had received from here. He saw three saloons, no different than a thousand others across the Southwest. Then he saw a more ornate sign on a newer building: *El Ranchero Saloon — Tom Clayson, Prop.* Clayson's name had appeared along with that of the Singara mayor in the letters.

Bob had now attracted attention. Men stared at the body and then at him, keeping abreast of Bob's horse. A man called back into a saloon and in a moment a dozen men stood on the porch, looking down at him as he passed.

Bob pulled in at the hitchrack of El Ranchero and tied both horses. He asked the staring swamper up on the porch, "Is Tom Clayson in there? Or Richard Rohlens?"

19

The man's eyes never left the body. "Both of 'em."

"Ask 'em to come out?"

The man nearly tripped over his mop bucket as he turned to the ornate doors. Bob waited, calmly studying the curious faces to either side of the rack. Two men appeared in the doorway and Bob swung under the rack to meet them as they hurried down the steps. "I'm Bob James."

The older of the two men, eyeing Bob and then the body lashed on the horse, said, "I'm Dick Rohlens. This is Tom Clayson."

Bob indicated the growing crowd. "Maybe we'd best get some place I can talk."

Clayson, a square-jawed, handsome man about Bob's age, said, "The new jail, Dick? That'd be best."

"You're right. Ride around the turn yonder, James. You'll see the new jail and office to your left."

Bob ducked under the rack again and pulled away with his grim burden. He spurred the horse to a fast trot, leaving the crowd behind. The moment he rounded the curve in the street, he saw the sign on a new, thick-walled, stout adobe structure.

"Sheriff," he read and he thought wryly, "I'm sure starting in business right away."

He reined in before the building with its

thick, stout door. The recessed windows were barred and their glass still had a new glitter. He found that the door was locked. He peered in a closed window, saw a new desk, smooth floor; it was an empty room awaiting occupancy.

Clayson hurried up, panting slightly, "I have the keys. Dick's breaking up the crowd."

Bob indicated the men hurrying around the turn. "Not much luck."

He untied the body as Clayson flung the door wide and hurried back to help him. When Clayson saw the slack face, he looked shocked. "Sonora!"

"You know him?"

"Sure . . . but let's get him inside."

They placed the body on the floor before the desk and Clayson locked the door. Bob looked around the room at an empty rack that would later hold rifles, at half a dozen chairs as new as the whitened adobe walls, at the gleaming barred door that opened on a small corridor.

Clayson interrupted his examination. "Where'd you find Sonora?"

"He found me last night in Phoenix and again this morning in that tangle of hills."

"He found you? But . . . he's dead."

"I shot him."

21

A heavy pounding on the door swung Clayson around. He cracked the door, then swung it wide and Rohlens and another man pushed in. Bob had a glimpse of the curious on the porch and around the hitchrack before Clayson closed and locked the door again.

Rohlens stopped short when he saw the dead man. "Why, that's Sonora Richards!"

"He shot him," Clayson said.

"He tried a bushwhack," Bob curtly answered the question in the eyes of all three men. He told how Sonora had sought him out the night before and then of the morning's fight. Bob finished, "So he knew I was going to be a lawman and he waited for me. I'd like to know why."

Rohlens slowly shook his head. "So would I. But the main thing is, we hired you to break up the outlaws and even before you get to town you bring in one of 'em."

"Richards?"

"Sure as shooting, though we have no proof. Hung around town, mostly, but he lived in an abandoned homestead shack ten miles or more north. Drunk and mean when he had money. When he didn't, Sonora would be missing awhile, but he'd always come back with money again. Seemed like there was always a holdup or robbery or rustling every time he was gone."

Bob showed Sonora's leather bag. "He had just a few dollars this time."

The third man broke his silence. "Maybe that's why he tried for you?"

Bob smiled crookedly. "Anyone knows a sheriff don't carry a full and bulging poke. He said his boss wanted him to make me welcome. He sure tried . . . but who was his boss?"

The three men exchanged blank looks and Rohlens scratched his head. "He never had a boss that I know of. He never worked a day all the time he was here — not legal work, anyhow. Know anything about it, Mort?"

The third man tugged at the short, black beard that fringed chin and jaw but shook his head. Clayson looked distastefully at the body. "Can't we get him out of here?"

Rohlens unlocked the door and admitted two men who looked sharply at Bob and then carried the body out.

"Sonora!" a dozen voices sounded as Rohlens closed the door. "The carpenter will fix a coffin. Did he have any kin?"

"Wife somewhere, I heard. But I've never seen her."

Rohlens dropped into a chair and surveyed Bob from boots to hat crown, his gaze lingering on holster and Colt, on deep chest and wide shoulders. He asked crisply, "Have you got the letter we sent you?"

Bob pulled the folded envelope from his shirt pocket and extended it. Rohlens read and returned the letter. He was a man in his fifties with a stocky body, big square hands and steady brown eyes. Gray hair streaked with black made a short crown above a broad and placid face. But strength lurked in the set of wide lips and formation of chin and jaw.

"I reckon we'd all better get acquainted, Bob, since we're the ones that hired you. You know I'm Dick Rohlens, town mayor as well as county commissioner. I own the hardware store down the street. This is Mort Jerris."

He indicated the bearded man, who extended his hand with a tight smile that held warmth nonetheless. He had a burring voice that suggested Scotland somewhere in the past.

"I manage the station for Wells Fargo, Bob. Running gold bullion and hard cash like I do, you're sure a welcome sight to me."

His fingers wrapped firmly around Bob's. Rohlens indicated the third man. "And Tom Clayson. Him and Mort are both county commissioners like me. Tom helps me run the town and keeps it oiled with his fine whiskey at El Ranchero."

Clayson chuckled as he shook hands. "That's my main job, Bob James. And you're welcome to sample it any time."

Bob liked the man. He stood tall and slender, neatly but not foppishly dressed in expensive white shirt, black silk string tie and sleeve garters of the same material. He gave the impression of coiled spring-steel muscles under the lithe ease of his body.

"I aim to get to that liquor business in a minute, Tom," Rohlens said. He looked at his two companions. "Well, you're looking at the gent we hired. He's more than a name and a letter now. Think he'll do?"

"He has my vote," Clayson replied instantly.

"He brought in Sonora Richards — dead. One outlaw less in Singara. We hired him to rid us of 'em," Jerris agreed. "What are we waiting for?"

Rohlens looked steadily at Bob. "You realize you signed a temporary contract with us commissioners, Bob? It's good only to regular election next year. By then you can run for office on your own. You've got that clear in mind?"

"Right from the beginning."

25

"Good." Rohlens sobered into official dignity. "Tom, you and Mort be witnesses. Bob, raise your right hand. Do you swear to uphold . . . ?"

The oath given, Rohlens crossed to the desk and took a shining new star from the middle drawer. He pinned it on Bob's left breast, stepped back as though to admire it. He looked around at his friends.

"Thank God! at last we got us a lawman! Tom, do you reckon it's time to spread the news and celebrate?"

III

Bob's uncertainty completely vanished as they started a near triumphal march from the new office to El Ranchero Saloon. The curious still hung around the office when the four men emerged. Rohlens introduced the new sheriff of Singara and explained the Sonora Richards' shooting. Then all marched down the street, the crowd growing behind the four, with Bob the center of attention.

El Ranchero proved to be surprisingly elegant within and Bob instantly knew that it did not welcome ordinary punchers or drifters. Tom Clayson catered to the wealthy and important, the solid citizens, ranchers

26

and mine owners or men of note like Mort Jerris of Wells Fargo.

Bob saw the usual tables when he entered, but more costly and not as numerous as in the average saloon. Clayson obviously thought of comfort and room in which to move rather than the number of customers he could crowd into the place. Gold patterned silk papered the paneled walls. The sawdust on the floor was clean and fresh. Each curve of the highly carved and massive bar along one end of the big room reflected the light from crystal chandeliers hanging from the ceiling.

Several men at the tables looked up when the procession entered. The greater part of the street crowd stopped on the planked walk outside as though El Ranchero, no matter what the occasion, was select and forbidden ground. Bob was introduced around. The names and faces grew blurred, but he knew he would clarify and fit them into place later. This one owned that ranch, this another, and this one had the Cactus Mine, this one the Golden Buzzard. This man ran the freight line to Prescott and Phoenix. One dry-voiced little man with shrewd eyes proved to be the banker.

Rohlens told about Sonora, proclaimed again that law had come to Singara. Everyone flowed to the bar. Bob accepted hand-shakes, slaps on the back, congratulations, statements of belief in his ability, awed questions about the outlaws he had faced in faraway and dangerous Balado. A constant succession of faces and names swirled before and around him as word spread throughout the town and men came to see for themselves.

Clayson appeared out of the turmoil at Bob's side. He had a knack of being clearly heard through the hubbub. "A big day for us — maybe a long one for you? . . . Then let's head out. Your office first."

Bob followed as Clayson worked around the edge of the bar and down a short corridor that led to the rear of the building. They emerged in an alley and Clayson led the way toward the distant office. Bob heard the faint murmur of voices marking the curious crowd still before the saloon and was glad Clayson had avoided it.

They returned to the new office and Bob instantly saw the horses were not before the hitchrack. Clayson noted his sudden alarm. "I sent my swamper to take the mounts to the livery stable. They're fed and watered. Rest easy."

They went into the office and Bob hesitated before circling the desk and dropping into the chair behind it. Clayson watched him look slowly around, rub a hand over the edge of the desk and look up at the empty gun rack, the bare bulletin board. Clayson said, "All brand new. How does it feel, Sheriff?"

"Great — but it'll take getting used to."

"We just built it, all for you. Anything you need in the way of ammunition, rifles, Colts — or anything — get it at Dick Rohlens' store. He'll charge it to the county."

Bob walked to the barred door and stepped into the small corridor beyond. Two cells with barred windows stood to either side. He noted the solid bunks and thick walls and turned back, satisfied.

"You'll have 'em filled before long," Clayson said as he lounged in a chair and trimmed the end from a long slim cheroot.

Bob returned to his chair behind the desk. "All of you talk about trouble here. How long? And who?"

"That 'how long' part's easy. Sort of growed up to it for over a year. Then real bad for six months. Bad enough to need a sheriff."

"There's always need of law. The most peaceful town has its quarrels that can end in gun fights."

"Well, we had those now and then," Clayson admitted. "Up to a year ago Singara was maybe half this size. Then a couple of prospectors made gold strikes. That brought in more gold hunters and now there's half a dozen mines in the county. Ranchers moved in. They brought punchers and the mines brought workers. All of 'em brought business to Singara so the town's become a center for supplies and shipments."

"And that brought the renegades and outlaws."

"That's it. Now, bandits stop stages every month or so. Gold riders from the mines get killed and the bullion is stolen. Cattle are rustled. Dick Rohlens, Mort and I began to worry, so we looked around for a lawman. The real big ones, like the Earps or Hickok, cost too much even if we could get 'em."

"So I got the job."

"You're made for us, Bob. A deputy, sure, but we know what kind of a deputy is needed in your hell-brew part of New Mexico. We figure we still have in you an Earp or a Hickok. We've spread word about a fast-gun lawman coming in to take over."

Bob made a grimace, knowing someone always took up a challenge like that — always a gun that had to prove it was faster. Clayson did not catch the swift change of expression. He slapped hands down on the chair arms and pushed himself up. "So this is where you work. Let's go see where you'll live."

"About the outlaws?" Bob insisted.

"They'll wait until you get to them." Clayson waited by the door and Bob could do nothing but leave the office with him.

They turned north at the next corner. The new street was irregularly spaced with small houses, some frame and some adobe. At the far end of the street stood a slightly more spacious one with a red tiled roof and a porch supported by slim columns of adobe.

"That's it," Clayson said. "The county bought it from old Ramirez. We remodeled it some and furnished it. Yours rent free, like it says in the contract."

Clayson produced a key, unlocked the door and swung it open. He handed the key to Bob. "Welcome home, Sheriff."

Bob moved from room to room, increasingly pleased with each step. Soft sunshine poured in the western windows, playing on new, cheap but comfortable furniture. There was a front room furnished with rug, horsehide sofa, a table, lamp and two upholstered chairs. A small narrow hall led off it, opening upon two bedrooms, both furnished.

Clayson explained. "We figured two bedrooms, even knowing you're single. Belongs to the county for whoever is sheriff, now or years from now. You could have visitors, or get married."

"Or the next sheriff will be."

"That's right. Now, here's the kitchen." Clayson led the way to a spacious room, again plainly but completely furnished. He waved to a table before a window. "Sit down, Sheriff. I'll get something El Ranchero contributed instead of the county."

He opened a cupboard and placed glasses on the table as Bob sat down. He opened a second cupboard and Bob saw half a dozen full bottles of liquor. Clayson opened one. "County budget doesn't allow for such foofooraw but I figured you'll protect me as much as anyone else."

"Bribery," Bob grinned. "Thanks."

Clayson poured and they drank to one another. Clayson pointed out the window. "You can see the back of your office from here. Corral and shelter, too, if you want to keep your horse close. We figured you would. County pays for feed and livery, in case you haven't read the fine lines in the contract."

Bob stretched out his legs and looked around the room. "Hard to believe all this is for me."

"You'll earn it — maybe with bullets."

"I know. And that reminds me, you never answered 'who'." Clayson looked puzzled and Bob said, "Who are they? Who backs 'em? Where do they hang out?"

Clayson refilled the shot glasses. "Who? Just suspicions. Like Sonora Richards — he'd come and go, not working but had money. That kind of suspicion. No more. Drifters here and there all over the county, first one place then another. That's who they are for what it's worth."

"Lot of riding, seems like."

"I'd say so. Where do they hang out? . . . I don't know."

"They'd have to have some place where they'd feel safe," Bob insisted. "Some saloon or spot in town. Some ranch or hide-out."

"Nothing in town. There are three saloons besides El Ranchero. I know their owners and not one of 'em would want hardcases and gunslammers at his place. Men drift in and out, of course, all kinds. But there's no bunch that's always together day in and day out. I take it you mean loafers without jobs so far as anyone knows?"

"That kind. They hang out in one spot."

"Sorry, not in Singara."

"What other towns, then?"

"There's nothing between here and Phoenix or north to the Mogollon. West, there's Salome but that's out of the county. There's just Singara."

"Then they have to be here."

"All right, then . . . find 'em!"

Bob frowned and Clayson refilled the shot glasses, waited for him to speak. Bob pulled at an ear lobe as he stared thoughtfully out the window. "Outlaws, bandits and rustlers — all over the county, you say. They'll get together somewhere. There's bound to be some kind of organization. Otherwise, how do they know what shipment is going where, or when it's safe to rustle beef, or when and by what route a gold rider brings bullion to town? They have to know."

Clayson tossed his drink in a single gulp. "You scare the hell out of me! You're saying they have a center, a leader, aren't you?"

"I'm guessing by what I've learned down in New Mexico."

"I don't believe it! Not in Singara! There's not a man anywhere in the county like that. But — it'd *have* to be in town, wouldn't it? And someone who hears everything that goes on — someone important?"

"That's right. So I thought of the saloons. They're clubs. Men ride in and out. They talk of this and that."

Clayson paced in agitation back and forth.

"No! Sure, we saloon keepers aren't exactly lily white in our reps, compared to a rancher, merchant or miner. But I know the other three as well as myself. They're honest men and we want a peaceful, lawful town as much as the preacher or the school teacher. No!"

Bob placated in an easy tone. "I'm not accusing. It's just something I have to ask before I even start my job. And the job looks harder and harder."

Clayson lost his worry with a laugh. "That's certain! Well, I've stayed too long. You'll want to eat and rest. Victuals are in the cupboards. You'll find 'em. I'll be getting on."

"I'll go with you to the livery stable. I have a saddle roll."

Much later, the meal over and the few dishes washed, Bob carried the lamp into the hall and made his choice of bedrooms. Undressed, he blew out the lamp and slipped into bed, bone weary and certain he would sleep. But it would not come and he looked up into the darkness, keenly aware of all the distant sounds in this strange town. It's home now, he reminded himself and he stretched out a long arm to touch his shirt on the chair beside the bed. His fingers caressed the metal of the new star and a strong surge of pride made him more wide awake than ever.

He swung long legs out of bed and lifted the blind at the window. He looked toward his own office. His eyes sought the faint shape of the dark building but it was too far off in the night to see.

But it was there, like the badge . . . his, if he proved himself.

IV

Bob first became familiar with Singara itself, going into its stores and meeting its people. Wherever he went, there was still talk about Sonora Richards. He learned from the carpenter that the body had been claimed. "Curt Hochner and a rider came in with a buckboard."

"Who's Hochner?"

"Runs a baling wire outfit 'way north of town. Just getting by, I'd say, though Hochner ain't the man to let you know if he's starving or wealthy."

"Richards worked for him?"

"Damned if I know. Hochner just said he'd take care of it."

Bob made a mental note to ride out to the Hochner spread as soon as he could. He visited the three saloons Clayson had mentioned, met their owners and saw some of their customers. The owners seemed genuinely glad to know that law had come at last. Bob agreed with Clayson that none of them would knowingly make his place a renegade hide-out.

In each saloon he bought drinks for the few customers gathered on a workday afternoon. He gathered information about each man and also about the county so that he began to have a mental map of the area wherein he would ramrod the law.

He wrote letters to the sheriffs of the adjoining counties, introducing himself and offering full cooperation in any pursuit of wanted men. He talked to merchants and realized the county truly boomed as Clayson had said.

He stopped in the Wells Fargo station and Mort Jerris made him welcome. "We want you out to the house for supper — me'n my wife and daughter. They want to meet you, like every lady in town does, I reckon."

"Be glad to as soon as I can get things in shape."

"Even before that, Bob. This might be a man's country but a wife more'n not can bring her husband around to thinking her way."

"I never thought of it that way. Balado

had mighty few married ladies. Most were of the other kind."

"But Singara's bigger and more settled. We got respectable ladies and a church that's alive and active. Mrs. Jerris and me belong. So does Madge, my daughter. Bet you by next week sometime you'll be invited to a social."

"I'm not much with that kind of thing," Bob protested.

Jerris' smile lightened his dark face. "Then figure on learning how to slick up for the ladies. They can't vote but their husbands do, and by next year's election the women can help or hinder."

Jerris, proud of his station, showed Bob around. In the big yard and stables workers greased axles on a stage coach and checked springs, pins and running gear. Bob admired the horses in their stalls and Jerris introduced him to a driver, Jim Hanlon.

"Glad to see a lawman," Hanlon said. "I was hit three weeks ago on the Ehrenburg run. Lost strongbox and my passengers' cash and watches."

"I'd like to talk to you about that. Say over a drink next door?"

Jerris nodded permission and a few moments later, at a corner table, Hanlon frowned at Bob's question. "Sheriff, you know how much one man looks like another with a bandanna over his face. About all you can see is the muzzle of the Colt he's holding. It's bigger than the man behind it."

"How many held you up last time?"

"Three. But that means nothing. Talk to the drivers of the other coaches, or the gold riders. Sometimes there's one, sometimes half a dozen. How many would it take to rustle a beef herd? A dozen?"

"All the same bunch, you'd say?"

"How you gonna tell? But everytime there's something valuable moving — coach, freight wagon, gold rider or beef — word gets to 'em. Of course, might be there's just a hell of a lot of scattered renegades. The Golden Buzzard was robbed — the strongbox blown right in the mine office. I heard at least ten was in on that. You're going to earn every cent they pay you for wearing that badge."

"I believe you."

The batwings swung open and two men entered. One was almost six feet tall and looked to weigh two hundred or more. His companion, a shadow beside him, was thin and angular, with a pinched face. Hanlon indicated the big man with a slight nod. "That's Curt Hochner. Some say he's one."

"I heard."

Hanlon looked at the clock. "Better get back to the station seeing I'm drawing Mort's pay. Thanks for the drink, Sheriff."

"Thanks for the talk."

"That's about it — talk, guesses. But, like I said, I'm sure glad there's a sheriff around now."

After a while Bob turned so he could watch the two men at the bar. They talked to the bartender. Bob noted their unwashed Levi's and shirts, dusty and decrepit hats. Hochner's boots had worn slantwise at the heels. But the guns in their holsters and the cartridges in the loops of their gun belts were metallic bright. After a second drink, the thin man hurried out, leaving Hochner to signal a third for himself.

Bob walked easily to the bar. Hochner caught his reflection in the back mirror and turned. He had a strong bone structure under the doughy flesh of his face. Small eyes rested on Bob's badge and lifted in surprise.

"Sheriff! Since when?"

"A few days ago. I'm Bob James."

Hochner eyed his extended hand then swiped his on his Levi's before he accepted the gesture. "Curt Hochner."

"I hear you run a ranch north of here."

"That's right — if you can call it a ranch." Hochner's voice, heavy as his body, had a subtle oily quality. "It's hell's own job getting started in beef."

"So they tell me. I missed meeting your friend."

"Jowett? He works for me, that is when there's something to do. Mostly for meat, beans and a drink now and then. About all I can afford. But Jowett says it's better than drifting."

"Some say Sonora Richards worked for you."

"Work? That one! He just hung around now and then until I'd get tired and boot him out. He jumped a feller a few days back and caught a bullet, so he ain't no bother now."

"He jumped me. Any idea why?"

Hochner's eyes skittered away and he shrugged big, powerful shoulders. "To rob you, maybe. Get your horse. I had little truck with Sonora. Never even seen his place after he took over that old shack."

"How'd he make a living?"

"Sheriff, I'll sure guess with you."

Bob signaled the bartender to give Hochner another drink and walked out. On the porch, a thought struck him and he waited until Hochner emerged. The big man hesi-

41

tated a split second at the batwings, then boldly stepped out on the porch.

Bob said pleasantly, "Speaking of Sonora, didn't I hear you took his body?"

"And buried it, for that matter. His wife was all broke up and had no way of taking care of things."

"Is she still out there?"

"Not if I know her. She never liked this country. Ain't seen or heard of her. She'll be on her way back where she come from by now. Well, I got to get along."

As Jerris had predicted, Bob came under the scrutiny of the ladies of the town. He met them in the stores and always touched his hat brim in answer to their curious stares. Mrs. Rohlens made a point to speak to him in her husband's hardware store. She was not really a large woman, but she was an assured one with the dignity, confidence and general formation of a pouter pigeon, accented by a huge hat adorned with bird wings and flowers. She pierced him with steel-blue eyes and tapped his arm with a folded fan.

"I approve of you, young man. Mr. Rohlens made an excellent choice. I'll tell him."

She marched away down the aisle like a queen.

Two nights later, he met Mrs. Jerris when Mort took him home for supper. She proved to be a wiry little woman with a long nose, flashing eyes and a surprisingly warm voice that made him feel instantly welcome.

He met Madge Jerris. She had her father's dark hair, thick, soft and blue-black, piled high on a proud head. She had violet eyes that grew deep when she was introduced and her smile was a slow move of thin, dark red lips. She moved with a grace that enhanced her full figure and Bob had difficulty in keeping his eyes off her as she sat across from him at the table. Twice he missed something Mort or Mrs. Jerris said and they had to repeat.

The meal finished, Mrs. Jerris promised cake and coffee and her daughter helped her take the dishes to the kitchen. They moved back and forth between the two rooms while Mort and Bob remained at the table. Mort left to get a cigar and Bob heard the murmur of voices from the kitchen.

". . . quiet man, ain't he?" Mrs. Jerris asked.

"He's very nice. So tall and handsome. I like —"

Someone closed the door and Mort returned. Bob's neck grew red. Yet he was pleased and felt a stir of excitement. A man would want a girl like Madge Jerris to approve of him.

After supper there was general talk. Mrs. Jerris and Madge were curious about his past. At last Bob knew he had stayed his time and reluctantly prepared to leave. He thanked Mrs. Jerris and Mort and then turned, hat in hand, to Madge.

She held out her hand and he awkwardly took it. He felt a tingle from her warm, soft fingers. She said, "Do come back, Sheriff. Please do."

"I will. Thank you. I will."

Well along the night dark street, he stopped and looked back at the glow of lamps through the window. He savored the evening and thoughtfully pursed his lips. He finally walked slowly toward Singara's main street to make his rounds.

He looked back again but couldn't see the Jerris' lights anymore. It didn't matter. She wanted to see him again and he recalled the shred of conversation he had heard before the kitchen door closed. His mind moved vaguely into the future.

He grinned and spoke softly to himself. "Suppose I do all right and I'm elected regular sheriff next year? Do you think . . . ?

Well, ain't impossible, is it?"

The memory of Madge Jerris' eyes, lips and figure stayed with him as he made the circuit from El Ranchero to the cheapest saloon and back to his new office. He settled down in his chair, well fed and warmed by thoughts he couldn't chase from his mind.

By morning he logically saw his position as it really was — a sheriff on probation. Folks liked him, and bringing in a dead Sonora Richards had done him no harm. But so far as Singara was concerned Bob couldn't ride forever on that bit of luck and his Balado reputation. Sooner or later, events would force him to prove his right to the badge. He must find some means to force the outlaws into the open and to jail.

He looked along the main street as he unlocked his office door. It had a weekday early morning peace. He entered his office and considered his main problem, wondering how he could get hold of some lead to the renegades. Curt Hochner? He might ride out and look around. Maybe here in town . . . if he kept watching and asking questions. But that was almost as bad as —

His eyes flicked first to a window as he saw someone ride past and then turned to the door to see the rider go on by. He heard a faint sound at the hitchrack beyond his line of vision through the open door. He heard slow steps across the wooden porch.

The stranger suddenly stood in the doorway. The bright morning sun in the street beyond revealed a tall silhouette, long legs, slender torso, a wide-brimmed hat and something slightly out of kilter that Bob could not quite place.

"Looking for me?" he asked.

The stranger stepped inside and Bob knew what had been wrong with the silhouette. Hair fell from under the hat over slender shoulders — long, bronze-red hair that had trapped the sun. He sat transfixed as he realized the Levi's, boots, shirt and jacket covered the body of a woman. Wide-spaced, sea-green eyes regarded him in steady speculation. She had a long oval face, its length accented by delicate, high-planed cheeks and a slightly pointed chin. The sun had tanned her and her long lips, beneath a straight ridged nose, made a dark red contrast.

Bob jerked to his feet. "Ma'am, I didn't know — Excuse me!"

He pushed a chair forward. Her steady gaze never wavered as she hesitated and then slowly sat down. Her chin held a stubborn angle as she slowly studied him from boots to crown of bare head.

She spoke in a drawl that could only have come up the trail from Texas. "So you're the sheriff they hired?"

"That's right. I'm Bob James."

The sea-green gaze literally speared him. "Did you kill a man the day you came to town?"

"Why . . . yes. He tried to bushwhack me."

She settled firmly in the chair. "Don't matter what he did. That's more'n well over now."

"Well . . . then . . . ?"

"Point is, *you* killed him and he was my husband. Seeing as I'm left widowed and with a lone dollar to my name, what are you going to do about me, Bob James?"

V

Bob's jaw dropped. "What!"

"Me . . . what are you going to do about me?"

"But . . . but, Sonora was outlaw and he tried —"

"I know what he tried. Outlaw he was and I don't deny it. But I'm a widow and I'm not outlaw; never was nor will be. So why should I go hungering and wandering?"

She met his gaze, directly and calmly. Through his confusion he became aware of

47

her striking, bold beauty and aware that more hid beneath rough and worn man's clothing.

He folded his hands on the desk, forced a smile and spoke reasonably. "Mrs. Richards, I don't think you understand this whole thing."

A lovely red brow arched with all the effect of a spoken denial of his statement and she needed no further protest.

"Look, sometimes a lawman has to shoot in line of duty. You understand that . . . ? Good! Then he's not to blame and the county's not to blame. An outlaw takes a gamble and he loses. That's his bad luck, in a way, and —"

"I'm not outlaw. I didn't gamble. Sonora did. I've got some kind of justice coming, seems to me."

His fingers interlocked tightly so that knuckles made a sharp pressure on one another. He held his explanation to a steady, even pace, a logical pressure that could not be brushed aside.

She didn't try. She sat there. Listening. Or did she? Sunlight glinted on deep waves of red hair, touched tanned cheek and dark red, immobile lips. Eyes blinked but never wavered. He read accusation in them as he brought up argument after argument. Not

48

accusation of murder, or killing her husband — he sensed she considered that a gain. But she did accuse him of casting her on a merciless world, not caring if she went cold or hungry.

Sweating slightly, he tried another line of argument. She was not his responsibility! Nor the law's, the city's, the county's. It was no one's responsibility. She should know that. She uncrossed and recrossed booted legs. He dropped back in his chair, baffled. He had made no apparent impression.

Her eyes blinked but didn't waver from his face, quietly accusing and demanding. He began to watch his fingers as he talked. From somewhere deep inside came the first touch of unwarranted guilt. He defended himself against a killer, that's all. He was sheriff . . . maybe not then wearing the badge but already hired for the job.

He emptied of argument. His voice slowed down, stopped in mid-sentence and for a long moment they looked at one another across the desk. She sighed. "You ain't said what you're going to do about me."

His hand loudly smacked down on the desk. "Nothing. Not a damn thing! I don't have to. So there it is. I'm doing nothing."

The calm, lovely face did not change

49

expression and the throaty voice with the Texas drawl asked, "Nothing?"

"Nothing. Sorry I lost my temper, Ma'am. But that's it. Nothing."

Her lips formed a faint smile. She looked welded to the chair and her voice confirmed it. "Want to bet, Bob James?"

He stared, thunderstruck and then exasperated, beyond anger. "Ma'am, I'm going to have to ask you to leave."

"Sure . . . ask."

His mouth hung open a moment, snapped shut. He read silent defiance, a dare to physically throw her out, just as silent a promise he'd have a fighting wildcat on his hands and the whole town out on the street as witness. He couldn't do that. But he couldn't let her stay. He had no intention of taking care of her.

"But you did kill her husband," the thought nagged and tugged at him. "How do you think she feels sitting there looking at you?"

Sweat made his palms sticky and trickled at the roots of his hair. He realized what this woman's presence could do to his job. What would the ladies of Singara say when they learned he had helped this beautiful redhead to find a house, say, or bought her a meal, or clothing? He had a frightening picture of Madge Jerris.

But there sat the redhead, unmoving and immovable. Bob took a deep breath. "Mrs. Richards —"

"I don't like the sound of that, Bob James. Now Sonora's gone, I might be Verda Carr again, what I was before I married. Sounds better, don't it?"

"Mrs. Carr — Richards — however you want it!" He calmed his voice. "There's no law forces me to do anything about you. But I will pay your stage fare to wherever you want to go. It might come out of my own pocket but since it was your husband I —"

"Won't come out of your pocket since you won't be paying it. There's no place that wants me or where I want to go. Singara's as good a place as any."

"But you have no money! No place in town!"

She moved then, a slow lift of body out of the chair. She walked to the barred door just beyond the desk, looked down the short corridor and then returned to her chair. "Since you're so all-fired legal, you could arrest me and I could stay in one of those cells. They're clean. More than I could say for the shack where we lived."

"You mean it!"

"Of course I do. What about it? If I'm a prisoner, no one can argue."

Bob shook his head. She again had possession of the chair and intended to stay there. Protest, anger, argument whirled around in Bob's mind but no words came out. He had to escape from her to think this thing out. He stood up.

She brightened. "That idea's all right?"

"I don't think so . . . Of course not! . . . Look, I have to see someone down the street."

"Go ahead. I'll wait."

He glared, muscles uncontrollably bunched preparatory to throwing her out bodily. But caution ruled and he grabbed his hat from the desk and lunged to the door. He recognized her mount at the hitchrack, Sonora's horse and saddle from which hung a partially filled flour sack. He sensed it held all her possessions.

Her voice carried out to him. "Take your time, Sheriff. I'm not going anywhere."

He fled up the street. He caught the curious glance of a passing rider and realized his long, hurried stride revealed his turmoil. He slowed his pace and continued to the curve of the street. What could he do with the woman back there?

At the curve, his eyes lighted on El Ranchero and he saw it as a haven. The saloon would have few if any customers this early in the day. He could have a much-needed drink and think. Besides, Tom Clayson — No, he decided. Get that tall redhead out of the office and town by yourself. Unless, of course, Tom might have some helpful idea.

A few moments later, Tom himself poured Bob's drink at the ornate bar. "Never saw you in this early before."

"Sort of upset."

"This'll settle things, all right. Eat something didn't set right?"

Bob wished Clayson would leave him alone. But the man was in a mood to talk and didn't notice Bob's impatience. "You've been visiting around and talking polite to the ladies, Bob."

"How do you know?"

"Not much happens in town doesn't find the news of it right in here."

Bob toyed with the whiskey glass. What would he do with that woman? She wouldn't leave town, but she must have kin somewhere who'd see she had a new start. She couldn't stay in the jail. Maybe he should risk a fight with her and just throw —

"You're a million miles away," Clayson's voice cut in and Bob started.

"Sorry, Tom."

"I was saying I heard you've been talking to drivers and such that were robbed. Get any help from 'em?"

"Nothing. Except Curt Hochner keeps coming to my mind. He's the kind of man who just might be part of the set-up."

Clayson laughed. "Don't go by that. I once knew a man who looked so mean and hungry you'd figure he'd knife you for a dime. Was worth half a million, I guess."

Bob shrugged. "He claimed he had nothing to do with Sonora. The man just hung around sometimes."

"Drifters do that — and loafers. No one ever saw Sonora working. He lived not too far away."

"So Hochner said. He buried the jasper to help out the wife."

Clayson sighed and his fingers softly tapped the bar. "Now there's a real beauty! She came into town a couple of times with Sonora. I wonder how a man like him ever persuaded her to marry him."

"I wonder, too."

"But you've never seen her!"

Aware of Clayson's puzzled look, Bob knew he had said too much and he also knew that he couldn't solve his problem by himself. Clayson could help. Suddenly Bob wondered how many had seen the woman come into his office and now wondered why he had fled and she remained.

"I've seen her, Tom. Just now. She's down at the jail waiting for me to come back."

"Mrs. Richards!"

Bob told the story of the woman's amazing, brazen demands. Clayson listened, at first astounded and then crinkles appeared at the corners of his eyes and lips. When Bob finished, Clayson could no longer control his burst of laughter.

"She . . . wants you to . . . take care of her!" he gasped and then burst into laughter again. "Tuck her in cozy at night and . . ."

He saw Bob's scowl and he sobered. "I'm sorry, Bob. But you see how funny it sounds?"

"It'd be funnier if she was a hundred miles away right now. There she is. I — we have to do something about her."

"You need another drink."

They stood silent for long moments, Bob unable to think of anything, hoping Clayson might have an idea. Clayson dashed his hopes by saying, "A hell of a thing, Bob. The only thing I can think of . . ."

"Yes?!"

"Put her up at the hotel, at least until tomorrow. By then she might agree to leave town. Or we can figure something."

Clayson's idea was a good first move. Bob pushed away from the bar. "I'll talk it over with Dick Rohlens. Might be she's right in wanting to stay in Singara, given half a chance to get started."

"I doubt it," Clayson said quickly. "She married trouble and she's probably trouble herself. There'll be just another Sonora Richards later on. Let that happen somewhere else."

Bob felt more confidence when he returned to his office. Verda Richards still sat before the desk but she looked up expectantly as he stepped into the room.

"All right, Mrs. Richards. Come with me."

"Where?"

"The hotel."

She arose. "Well, sounds like you're being reasonable."

"Don't gamble on it."

She smiled, face and eyes glowing. "Reckon I can decide about that, Bob James."

He let her go through the door before him. As she passed, he had the full impact of the sea-green eyes. They held and studied him for an instant before she stepped out on the porch. In that second she was not all brash, confident and stubborn demand. The eyes had held a glow of gratitude and also the shadow of fear. She hid desperation.

He steeled himself against that thought. She walked with an innate grace that belied the rough clothing. She looked straight ahead, lips firm and head high. She carried her battered hat in her hand and her hair was a magnificent red-bronze cascade down her shoulders, a glowing contrast to the coarse blue material of her jacket. And she was as tall as himself, Bob thought with faint surprise.

A buckboard rattled around the turn toward them. The driver pulled the horse down to a slow walk, stared, shifted curious eyes from Verda Richards to Bob, whose neck reddened.

The driver leaned out from the buckboard seat. Verda Richards' chin came up as the man eyed her from head to foot. He said, "Morning, Sheriff."

"Morning," Bob answered shortly.

The man wanted to stop but had no excuse. The buckboard moved slowly by but Bob could feel the weight of the speculative, shocked eyes between his shoulders. Mrs. Richards had high color on her cheeks.

They rounded the turn and the hotel stood far ahead. The street, thankfully, was empty of traffic, the hitchracks bare. For a moment Bob felt more at ease. Then he saw the milliner just within her shop doorway. She looked in frozen shocked curiosity as they passed. A man came out of the gunshop, halted in midstride and leaned against the building. The man's eyes rested speculatively on Verda Richards and then knowingly on Bob. He made a hardly perceptible nod and smile that made Bob want to hit him.

They came to the hotel. In the empty lobby, she seemed about to speak but instead looked away, lips twisted angrily, as Bob rang the bell. The clerk appeared through a door behind the counter, expectancy changing to quickly concealed shock as he saw Verda.

"A room for the lady," Bob said gruffly, then added, "Meals included for the time she'll stay."

The clerk slowly turned the register and extended the pen. As she bent to the register, the clerk looked over her head at Bob. He turned the register and asked as he noted the room number, "You'll be alone, Ma'am?"

Her face turned scarlet. "How else should I be!"

The clerk saw Bob's angry scowl and stumbled on. "Of course. It's something you sort of ask everyone without thinking . . .

That's all . . . Sorry. You're Room Five. Looks out over the street. How long will you be here, Ma'am?"

"Not long," Bob answered.

The clerk extended a key. "Up the stairs and to the front of the building, Ma'am."

She turned to Bob. "Thank you. This helps. Maybe I can pay back someday."

She turned to the stairs and disappeared. Bob started to leave but the clerk checked him. "Sheriff, that's Sonora Richards' wife."

"*Was.* He's dead. What about it?"

"I just work here. Joe Willets owns the place but Mrs. Willets runs it. Understand?"

"Get to it."

"Well — her. No dress, just something maybe her husband wore. No carpetbag or trunk. She ain't got money for the room or the meals, Sheriff. Who's to pay."

"I will," Bob snapped and dropped money on the counter. "That's to make you and the Willets feel safe. We'll settle up when she leaves — maybe tomorrow's stage, maybe next day."

"Thanks, Sheriff. Not my doing, like I said." He looked sly and smiled. "There's a back stairs if you need it. Just open the alley door and you can get —"

Bob grabbed his shirt front. The man squawked as he was lifted to the tip of his

59

toes. His face went white as his eyes rounded and his mouth gaped. Bob's right fist clenched, then opened and he pushed the man away. The clerk banged against the counter, stood fearfully plastered.

Bob rubbed his hands as though wiping off filth. He turned on his heel and strode out of the hotel.

VI

He stepped out on the street, looking at Clayson's El Ranchero, at Rohlens' hardware store and then up over his shoulder at the hotel, relieved that the redheaded woman was there instead of back at his office. He recalled the encounters along the street, the implications of the clerk. No matter where Verda Richards stayed, tongues would wag. That was always bad in these small towns and ever present. But to have it start now, at the very beginning of his work in Singara, would be real disaster.

When he mounted the steps of El Ranchero, Clayson waited for him on the porch. "I saw you take her to the hotel. She's sure man-tall but woman shaped."

"And trouble, like you said. People will talk plenty and fast — if it's not already started. Maybe we'd better tell Dick what's happened — and Mort Jerris, since he's a county commissioner."

"I'm stuck here until my bartender shows up. Want to wait for me?"

"Well, she's at least out of sight. I'll take care of her horse and meet you here."

He walked morosely back to the jail. He led her horse around the building to his own corral, off-saddled and turned it in. Bob swung the saddle up on a rail, first untying the flour sack. Angles and curves beneath the coarse sacking suggested small boxes, pieces of clothing — a pitiful summary of possessions.

He carried the sack to the office. He dropped into his chair behind the desk, glanced at the new clock and then looked unseeingly through the open door out on the street, thoughts slowly churning.

The clock ticked steadily, like his own brain over the problem. What in the world could he do with an outlaw's wife? The full import of that struck him, realizing her sudden appearance and demands had blinded him to an unexpected opportunity. He sat bolt upright.

If Sonora Richards rode with the outlaws, then his wife would know the renegades! Bob struck his head with the heel of his hand. He'd be a fool to pack her off out of town without questioning her.

Bob stood up, face alight. He heard the sound of hooves and wheels, glanced again at the clock. That would be the stage from Ehrenburg and Salome. The sounds grew louder. A strident voice called, "Sheriff! James! Where in hell's the sheriff!"

He jumped out on the porch. The stage had pulled into the hitchrack, the six horses snorting, tossing heads, blowing. Bob saw the sweat streaking their flanks, the foam at their mouths. He saw a long, raw scar on the coach that only a bullet could make. Hanlon, at the reins, said tightly, "Holdup. Ten of 'em. They got Joe and a passenger. They're inside."

The coach door slammed open and a woman jumped out, sobbing in fright and shock. Bob saw two slack forms inside, one on a seat and one on the floor. The woman, stout and gray-haired, looked about. Her rounded eyes centered on Bob's badge.

"Thank God!"

She turned paper white, started to collapse. Bob grabbed her and her dead weight almost pulled him down. Hanlon had jumped from the high seat. At the same moment, men raced around either end of the coach, one of them shouting, "What's wrong? What's happened?"

Bob eased the woman to the ground. He speared a finger at one of the men. "You! Get a doctor. Hurry!"

"Holdup!" the man's face blanched. He turned on a heel and raced away.

Other townspeople streamed along the street, converging on the coach. Hanlon and Bob jumped to the open door. Bob pulled up on the step to look at the man on the floor. He saw a big stain on the right shoulder, a tanned, deeply, wrinkled face, pale now with loss of blood.

"Blaine — he's the shotgun guard," Hanlon said. "They were hidden up in the rocks and they took Blaine out with the first shot. Four waiting ahead for me."

Bob turned to the man lying limp on the seat. "This one?"

"Drummer from California. He tried to save his wallet. Stomach shot. I don't know if he'll live or not."

Bob dropped back to the ground and faced the gathering crowd, his body blocking view into the coach. "Scatter out, now. Nothing you can do. Give the lady air. The doctor's coming. Back up, now." In an aside to Hanlon, "Get Mort Jerris down here."

He closed the coach door and bent over the woman. Her eyes fluttered and she looked blankly up. Recognition and memory flooded her and she grabbed Bob's arms, clinging tightly. He lifted her to her feet and took her inside the office. Two riders raced around the far curve of the street, the doctor and Mort Jerris thundering up side by side. Both men vaulted out of the saddles, the doctor to race toward the coach and Jerris to the office.

He startled the woman whom Bob had seated. She gave a half scream and seemed about to faint again until Bob explained Mort and his position. Jerris gave the woman a few polite but impatient minutes and then turned to Bob. "Hanlon told me. Joe Blaine and a passenger hit. The strongbox taken. A hell of a thing! This lady?"

"All nerves right now, but all right," Bob assured him. "Did Hanlon come back with you?"

"On his way."

Bob turned to the woman. "Just rest back easy, Ma'am. It's all over and you're safe. I'll be right outside if you need me. All right?"

He smiled tightly at her nod and hurried out to the porch. Blaine had been lifted out and lay on the porch, eyes closed and face white. Doc Laren crouched inside the coach, working over the man on the seat.

Bob pushed his head in the coach. "What's

the damage?"

"Blaine out there has lost blood and has a bullet-broken shoulder. He'll live. But this'n . . . I don't know. Leave me be."

Bob turned to Jerris and they walked back to the boot of the stage. The tarpaulin hung loose and they saw the luggage of the woman and the drummer. The strongbox was missing and Jerris grunted a painful acceptance of disaster.

The doctor emerged from the coach, shaking his head, as Bob and Jerris returned to the porch. "I'd give two cents and no more for that man's life. That forty-four slug tore him up. Think you can rig up a couple of stretchers and get him and Blaine to my place?"

Bob picked four men, sent two others scurrying to the lumber yard for poles. Hanlon came up and Bob waved him and Jerris inside. Within ten minutes the two wounded men were carried gently down the street, the doctor pacing beside the stretchers. Bob assigned a woman in the crowd to see that the lone unscathed passenger reached the stage station where another coach would take her on to Phoenix.

Finally Bob stepped in his office and closed the door. He sat down behind his desk and spoke to Hanlon. "Tell me about it."

The driver quickly outlined what had happened. Jerris asked about the strongbox. Hanlon replied, "They had a pack horse ready for it. So they'll have toted it somewhere out in the desert before they open it."

Bob learned that Blaine, sharp-eyed as a shotgun guard should be, had spotted the first lurking rider, but too late. Hanlon said, "Another'n Blaine didn't see up in the rocks shot him. The drummer would be all right but he had to try for a derringer he carried in his pocket. It was planned slick, Sheriff, only Blaine and that drummer messed it up."

Bob stood up. "Hanlon, you and Mort will ride with me. I'm making up a posse. Get horses. We'll ride in fifteen minutes."

The crowd still milled around the coach. Hanlon and Jerris climbed in the seat and drove off as Bob enlisted at least twenty likely looking men and swore them in as deputies. They scattered for their horses and guns.

Tom Clayson hurried up. "Heard the news, Bob. Anything I can do?"

"If you can ride and shoot, yes. I'll deputize you."

"Count me in."

The posse gathered. Bob signaled Hanlon, Jerris and Clayson to ride with him and led the way out of Singara, west along the road toward Hope and Salome. Bob checked the eagerness of the posse, holding them to a ground-eating lope and trot.

Bob answered Jerris' grumble. "This could be a long, hard ride, Mort, before we catch up with those outlaws. I want our mounts fresh when we do. They'll be pushing fast and I'm counting on exactly that to wear out their horses."

Jerris saw the point and subsided. Bob asked him about the strongbox and its contents. "Hard, cold cash for the Singara bank, Bob. Currency and coin."

"How did they know it was on the stage?"

"They didn't!"

"You forget. They brought a pack horse. Someone knew."

"Damn it! How could they?"

Clayson edged his horse close. "They planned to hit the stage. Something could go wrong. So an extra horse for a wounded man would figure."

Bob shrugged. "Well, we're bound to find out."

Some twenty miles or so out, Hanlon pointed ahead to where low hills broke on either side of the road. The country was barren, open desert but Bob knew the apparently smooth sweep to distant mountains concealed gullies, swales and arroyos. They came into the place where the hills forced the road to wind erratically like a snake around boulder-strewn spurs of hills. They rode around two of the blind turns before Hanlon pointed just ahead.

"Right there."

The sign confirmed it. Bob saw where the stage horses had stood stamping impatiently, and he also found the tracks of the outlaws. Some of them had held guns on Hanlon and the wounded Blaine. He saw boot tracks, marking the outlaws who had thrown open the coach door, of three others who had gone to the boot. He saw the mark where one corner of the strongbox had dropped to the ground and had then been picked up again.

Bob ordered the posse to move out to either side of the road, casting in ever-widening circles. He found the first sign, where bandit horses had been held in a deep curve of rocks that concealed them from the road and the approaching stage. In very few moments, he picked up the trail. They had come in and left from the north.

Bob pointed it out to Jerris and Clayson.

"We follow the sign. It's not too old but still they got a jump on us."

Clayson looked along the line of bleak hills and then out on the desolate, empty plain. "They'll be riding fast and hard. They could be anywhere by now."

"And they got the bank money," Jerris added morosely. "Wells Fargo will sure be asking me all about that."

Bob turned to his horse. "With luck, we might get it back for them. So let's don't waste time."

The trail led north, skirting the hills for many miles. Just before the low range ended, the bandits struck away from the hills, riding east and north. Bob asked Jerris, "What's ahead?"

"Open country. Now and then a few hills. Then broken and rolling country that leads into the high mountains. Desert ends there."

"Towns or anything?"

"No. A couple of mines maybe forty miles from here. There's a couple of ranches, too." He pointed off to the south and east. "Singara over there."

"No hiding places, then?"

Clayson spoke up. "Plenty of them. You could camp a month in a deep arroyo and never be seen. But I figure they're headed for the high canyon country. If they make it, we'll have one chance in a thousand of finding 'em."

Bob tugged his hat brim lower over his eyes. "Nothing like trying."

He set spurs and the posse strung out behind him. Within a mile they came on an arroyo, hitherto invisible, yet a deep, dry streambed down which storm waters would roar from the distant mountains. The trail led down a broken bank into the trough and then followed its winding course for a couple of miles.

Rounding a turn, Bob first saw the box. Then Jerris saw it and, with an oath, spurred ahead. When Bob came up, Jerris had dismounted and looked angrily at the box. It was of thick metal, rectangular. A bullet-smashed lock hung from the lid, thrown back to reveal the empty interior. Bob saw the black lettering on its side, *Wells Fargo*.

"Gone," Jerris said needlessly.

The trampled earth about the box showed where horses had impatiently stood. Boot heel marks showed clearly. Bob dismounted and moved about, reading the signs. He returned to Jerris, Clayson and the circle of mounted possemen.

"They rode on down the canyon after seeing how much they got from the holdup. How much was it. Mort?"

70

Jerris threw a glance at the curious deputies. "More'n I care to think about. If we find it, you'll know. If not, I'll tell you in private."

Bob understood. Except for himself and Clayson, the men of the posse were uninvolved in this robbery. But hearing what this strongbox had carried, they could innocently enough tell others who would think such loot would be worth the risk of banditry. And who knows, Bob thought grimly, but what a posseman now might become a holdup man a week from now?

"Cash and currency, you said."

Jerris nodded. "Gold and silver coins, greenbacks and yellowbacks."

"They've put it in saddlebags," Bob decided, "so as not to be bothered by the box."

He swung back into saddle and went at a fast trot down the arroyo, eyes on the trail sign. Again the posse lined out behind him. A mile farther on, he saw a broken bank ahead and the outlaw trail led directly to and up it. It was a steep scramble but the horse made it to the rim above and, once more, open desert country spread vacantly for miles about.

Ten miles along, the trail, leading straight as an arrow, suddenly swerved to the north. Bob looked questioningly at Jerris and Clayson. Clayson pointed ahead. "Joe Blotkin's Rafter B over that way. This bunch took no chance on being seen."

"Where's Hochner's spread?" Bob asked.

Clayson pointed almost due south. "Twenty miles or more that way. Singara ten beyond. This trail's leading clean away from there."

Bob cast out the brief suspicion. The outlaws had pushed ahead hard and Bob increased the pace of the posse. He looked up at the sun, now just beyond the meridian and starting its long, slow arc to the west.

His eyes swept the horizon, keened to catch the first faint sign of dust plumes marking a band of riders. There was none and the county remained devoid of life. Yet the trail led straight on. Now he saw, far to the north, a faint purple line along the horizon that must mark the sanctuary of the canyon country.

He again increased the pace of the pursuit. He had to catch sight of the outlaws before they reached that haven. A line of low hillocks gradually lifted ahead and the trail led directly toward a break between them. The posse threaded the brief, shallow pass and Bob suddenly drew rein, lifting his arm as a signal to halt.

An irregular circle of hoof-pocked earth showed where the bandits had halted. Bob rode slowly forward, Jerris and Clayson to either side. Bob searched the area, eyes casting about. He settled back in the saddle.

"Well?" Jerris demanded.

"They bunched here. Then they broke up, each man riding for himself in a different direction. You can see . . . there . . . there . . . there . . ."

The sign showed clearly and, pointed out to them, both Jerris and Clayson could see it. Jerris choked, "What now?"

"They divided the money and split," Clayson said slowly. "Ten different trails."

Jerris' fist smashed down on the saddle horn. "This licks us!"

VII

Bob looked disconsolately at the out-fan of trails and then slowly looked in a wide circle around the empty horizon, fighting back a sense of defeat. To divide the loot and then leave each man for himself would be logical, but it didn't tie in with what little he knew about the Singara renegades. They were one organization, no matter how scattered their bands or depredations might be.

"This is an old trick to throw off a posse.

They scatter to erase trail and then meet again somewhere ahead."

Jerris asked with faint hope, "You mean we're not licked?"

"Maybe not yet." Bob considered the posse. "Mort, you and Tom know the country. Pick five men each. Take one of these trails and follow it. Same for you, Tom. I'll take Hanlon."

Clayson dubiously asked, "Suppose the sign fades out?"

"That's a chance, but I think they'll tie in. If you come on your outlaw before that happens, try to keep out of his sight. If you can't, arrest him. Avoid gunplay if you can. We'll want him able to talk."

"But suppose *all* our trails fade out?"

"In that case, we'll ride back to Singara."

Jerris and Clayson picked their men. Hanlon and four men moved to Bob. Jerris chose a trail heading due east and Clayson took one angling southeast. Bob looked toward the far line of mountains, now more distinct, and took one of the remaining trails leading in that general direction.

He led his men at a swift pace northward. Far to the south, Clayson's group vanished as it dropped into an arroyo. Some distance ahead, Bob saw another dry, wide and shallow bed. The trail he followed led directly to it.

They rode down into the rocky and gravelly arroyo, followed the gouging mark of horseshoes until the bandit sped up and over the far bank. Clear signs told that he rode fast and straight as though fearing no pursuit. Bob felt a grim pleasure. Let the man wear his horse out soon and be forced to rest! That worked in the posse's favor.

The miles sped by. The northern mountains grew higher and more distinct, a spiked barrier all along the horizon. Saguaro stood about like tall, dusty-green, crooked-armed sentinels who let the posse by without challenge. The sun dipped westward but still there was no sign of their quarry.

Bob hoped to find indications that the rider had joined the outlaws ahead or that this trail would change direction — either one a signal of the converging Bob hoped for. But miles continued to roll behind and neither happened.

They came on another arroyo, deeper and steep-banked. The outlaw had stood here for some minutes and then had moved slowly northward along the rim, as though looking for a way down into the miniature canyon below. Five miles along, another, shallow side-arroyo fed into the main one and it was easy to follow the bandit's sign down into it.

Suddenly all trail vanished. This arroyo was filled with gravel, with rocks and boulders of all sizes, rolled and tumbled by the wild waters that rushed through in flood time. Bob drew rein and studied the narrow streambed in both directions. He had a choice and one of them would be wrong.

Hanlon asked, "Which way you figure he went?"

Bob said nothing, mind busy. For five or more miles south, he knew there was no way up the cliff-like banks, for the posse had already come that way. The man must have headed north along the arroyo. It might pinch out up near the mountains or there might be more side-washes feeding into it, any of them easy exits. The mountains, Clayson had said, offered a bandit refuge a hundred times over.

Bob turned north. Boulders and rocks slowed the pace, yet Bob still pressed forward. Sunlight did not touch the posse though the sky was gold-bright above the rims. Hanlon moved up near Bob and the other four pressed close behind.

Bob covertly studied them. He led men for the first time in this Singara country and he looked at each for sign of questioning or mistrust. He found none. There was no reason for it yet. It depended on the end of this ride and search. If he failed . . . He shrugged off the thought.

The arroyo wound endlessly. Suddenly they came on a deep side-wash that sloped gently upward to the east. The last flood, maybe months before, had washed a fan of sand and silt down the side-wash into the main arroyo itself. It lay like a smooth carpet for fifty feet or more from wall to wall.

Bob drew rein, Hanlon beside him. He heard the men move restlessly behind but he dared not look at them. Not a mark on that carpet of sand! The outlaw could not have crossed it without leaving one nor could he climb the cliff walls.

Hanlon swiped his hand across his forehead. "Well, you lost him, that's sure."

Bob heard a stir among the men behind him. He said flatly, "That's right. It happens."

"Reckon it does, but what do we do now?"

"Back down the arroyo. If he didn't come this way, he went the other. Any better idea?"

"No, seeing as how there's nothing else."

Bob reined about and the posse turned. Bob caught a subtle new expression in the men's faces, something faintly withdrawn. Just the first touch of judgment? he wondered. Then they were lined out again and retracing their way south.

The light had perceptibly dimmed down in this minor canyon when they came back to the place where the outlaw had entered. Bob rode by with hardly a glance at the swale but the men gave it long, speculative looks and then threw covert glances at him. He witnessed the first small tarnish on his reputation and there was nothing he could do about it.

Rocks and boulders prevented trail signs and Bob rode blind. But he watched the banks to either side. They rode about a mile, rounded the third of the sharp bends and Bob saw the shallow wash coming in from the east. He reined in. Sharp scanning of the ground at first revealed nothing but then Bob saw, within the mouth of the wash, a newly scarred rock. A horseshoe had done that. He rode deeper into the wash. Soon sand and gravel appeared and immediately he saw the tracks.

Bob said to Hanlon, "The renegade knows the country real well. He fooled us for a while."

Hanlon shrugged as Bob led the way into the wash. It became more shallow, then widened and they had but to follow plain tracks. The outlaw had suddenly veered southward up out of the arroyo, then headed directly east.

The sun now sat low in the west and Bob set a faster pace. The miles sped by. Suddenly Hanlon pointed ahead to a vague line that broke the desert. "That's the Singara to Prescott road."

They came on it. The trail they followed plunged into the road. The dirt highway bore a thousand tracks, pointing both north and south. It had been churned and grooved by the wheels of coaches, buckboards and freight wagons. The track of one animal could not be distinguished from the rest. Bob finally inwardly admitted he had been licked.

He reined in. "How far to Singara?"

"Maybe twenty miles or a little more," Hanlon answered.

Bob looked northward toward the distant mountains. Twice the distance, he judged by their darkening jagged peaks low against the horizon.

"Our man circled to throw off trail and then headed for Singara. We'll find him there."

"Might take some doing," Hanlon guessed with a faint edge.

"Might — again, might not. My job, ain't it?"

"That it is . . . and I'm glad of it. Been a heap of riding today and I'm glad to head home."

Bob turned southward, silent and withdrawn. He knew Hanlon had almost added "for nothing" to his comment about riding and Bob couldn't really blame the man. It had been exactly that unless Clayson or Jerris had more luck. But Bob couldn't work up any hope on that score.

Approaching Singara from this direction, the desert floor gradually broke into a series of waves, steadily mounting in height. Bob wondered if this was the beginning of that monotonous series of hills where Sonora had tried to kill him. He suddenly asked, "Is the Hochner spread around here?"

"Not far," Hanlon answered in surprise. "If we strike off the road, it's about five miles, maybe six, south and west."

"Let's visit him."

The land became steadily more broken, swales deeper, and now hillocks appeared, set apart rather than the series of crests Bob had seen before. They grew larger and, rounding one of them, Bob saw a clump of palo verde and desert growth far ahead.

"Hochner's," Hanlon said. "Water's close

to the surface from here on to Singara. A man can run cattle if he drills wells and builds tanks."

There was no sign of cattle. The trees, cacti and bushes grew more distinct and individual. Then Bob saw the adobe buildings, all low and squat. The largest he judged to be the ranch house, though it seemed hardly roomier than the rest. He saw a corral and three horses.

Bob lifted his voice above the soft, steady sound of hooves. "Might be nothing here, but be ready for trouble. Don't ask for it. If there is, no gunplay until I start it."

The five men nodded. They had been seen from the house. Three men came out and stood looking toward the posse. They seemed to be no more than surprised and curious. Still, Bob loosened the Colt for a fast draw.

Hochner, Jowett and a mean-looking man waited as Bob and the posse rode into the area of littered sand that passed as a yard. The stranger with Hochner might be anything, Bob judged swiftly — puncher working at starvation wages, saddle bum in for a day or two before drifting on. All three might have worn bandanna masks this morning and shot two men in the course of a robbery.

He drew rein and the posse fanned out behind him. Hochner looked around and then up at Bob, his heavy face blank. "What's all this, Sheriff?"

"Just riding by and dropped in."

Hochner's cynical chuckle rumbled out of his barrel chest. "Neighborly of you, if I could believe it . . . seeing as you ride with five deputies."

"That part's law business. You're not, except if you could help us."

"Thought as much. How?"

"Had any visitors? Seen anyone riding by?"

Hochner gave each of his friends a slow and mocking look. "How about it? We been right here for three days but maybe somebody slipped in that we didn't see?"

"Not as I know of," Jowett drawled. "Been right lonesome 'round here."

Bob darted swift glances at the house, the barn and the corral. The unsaddled horses showed no signs of recent hard riding. He had the lawman's feel that the house and the other buildings were empty. Nor did Hochner and his friends show any tension or alarm.

Hochner sighed, "Now I declare, Sheriff. We ain't going to be a bit of help."

"Well, took the chance anyway." Bob

started to rein about, checked. "Ain't the Richards' shack close about?"

Hochner could not conceal surprise and slight wariness. He indicated direction with a move of his chin. "You hold that way toward the Singara road, you'll come on it."

Bob waved his thanks and rode off, the deputies following. After a moment, Hanlon rode up beside him. He jerked a thumb over his shoulder. "Hochner and them two ain't moved. Still watching us."

"I know Jowett. Who was the other?"

"Never saw him before that I remember. But he's the kind I'd watch close if I rode alone somewhere and met him. You figure he . . . ?"

"Not now. I saw nothing wrong back there and they answered questions straight enough. How do you figure?"

"You're right. But they look so plug-ugly mean!"

"A man I knew down in Balado," Bob said easily. "Tall and good looking. Smiled nice and talked nice. You wanted to like him. We hung him for five murders and robberies. Still talking nice and good looking up to the time we put the hood over his head."

Hanlon grunted, nothing more.

Not long after, Bob saw the single small shack ahead and off to the right. Like Hochner's place, the shack sat amidst scant palo verde and cacti. Bob saw the low wall of a well and the remains of what had once been an adobe outbuilding, all but the irregular foundation vanished.

He dismounted with a brief word to the men. The building, also of adobe, was hardly more than a long, narrow room. Windows stared blindly out at him, one of them holding dirty shards of broken glass, a burlap sack serving as protection from wind and sun. The door stood open and Bob stepped inside.

The place had the odor of unwashed clothes, greasy cooked foods, and dust. Objects gradually took shape — a table that looked as though it would wobble with the mere weight of a glance, a rusty stove and equally rusty pipe angled through a hole in the wall, two boxes that had served as chairs. Bob saw clothing hanging from pegs on the wall — Sonora's. He saw a cotton dress, worn to holes, discarded on one of the two narrow bunks. Empty shelves above the stove told a mute story of little food.

He rubbed his hand along his jaw, his eyes growing bleak. He could now understand why Verda Richards said a jail cell was cleaner and better. How, Bob wondered, could a man subject his wife to a place like this? He had a picture of Sonora as he had seen the man in the Phoenix saloon and began to understand.

An impatient voice called, "Sheriff? All right in there?"

Bob started out of his thoughts. "All right. Nothing here. Coming."

He gave the place a last, comprehensive look. No wonder that tall redhead wouldn't come back to this, or anything like it. Maybe this is all she has to turn to, here or anywhere else.

He stepped outside, blinking against the brighter light. He walked in grim thought to his horse and mounted.

VIII

The sun was far below the western hills when Bob and his deputies rode wearily into Singara. There had been little or no talk the last miles but there had been no need for it. Bob rode in without so much as a glimpse of an outlaw or of Mort Jerris' money. A dark sense of failure rode with him right up to the jail hitchrack. Jerris and Clayson waited for him and a single glance told Bob they had come in empty-handed, too.

He dismounted and said in a flat voice, "I guess that's all, gents. Thanks to each of you for helping out."

A voice called, "Didn't come to much, Sheriff."

"Don't be too sure. We'll find the money — and the outlaws. You'll be asked to ride again. Depend on it."

The deputies slowly moved away as Rohlens hurried up. Bob walked into the office and Jerris, Clayson and Rohlens followed him. Bob dropped his hat on the desk and eased into his chair. "You found no trail, Tom?"

Clayson shook his head and Mort Jerris growled, "Same goes for me. That bunch just split up and disappeared — the money with 'em."

Rohlens eyed Bob. "You figure it's gone for good?"

"Not if I can help it."

"Point is," Jerris said, "how can you help it?"

"A bunch of renegades has more money than they've ever had before at one time in their lives. I figure Singara has known 'em as drifters, chuckline riders, loafers. Men like that don't know how to handle money."

Clayson made an impatient sound. "Lot of guessing, and where does it get us?"

"Where? Suppose you ran one of the other saloons instead of El Ranchero. Suddenly you see a man gambling heavy and buying drinks for the house. Last time you saw him, he hardly had two dollars to rub together. What would you think, after this holdup? Or a drifter buys expensive horseflesh, a saddle, or flashy Stetson and tolled boots. A man like that would bear some questions."

Bob looked around. "Can you help me spread word to the merchants and ranchers to tell me if something like that happens?"

They nodded in unison. Clayson, eyes suddenly sharp, asked, "But that's just waiting. Is that all you do?"

"No. I'm riding out to where that trail split up. We tried to follow just three of 'em today. That leaves seven other trails."

Jerris made a soundless whistle. "That could mean a heap of riding!"

"Right now, I've done enough for one day. If the rest of you feel as dusty and hungry as I do . . ."

Jerris pulled a sigh from deep in his chest. "I guess you're right, Bob. See you in the morning."

Bob took care of his horse before trudging wearily home. He scrubbed off dust and grime in a big wooden tub and changed to fresh clothing. He went into the kitchen, noting that deep purple twilight had descended. He decided on a drink before cooking supper.

He didn't bother to light the lamp, there being just enough light to find liquor bottle and glass. He sat down at the table before the window, and swallowed a dollop of the fiery liquid. He looked musingly out the window, hardly aware of the distant lights here and there, marking twilight-hidden houses. He saw much more clearly the faces of the posse as he had dismissed it, heard the doubtful note in Jerris' voice and Clayson's questions.

Bob sipped the liquor again. It was a problem far worse than Balado's. There, at least, certain saloons and ranches were known as gathering places for suspicious characters. But Singara . . . Bob saw the trail breaking up and fanning out. He saw the empty strongbox but a deep instinct told him the money had not been divided. It had gone to some cache or unknown headquarters. Maybe not a headquarters as such, just as there was no one loafing place in Singara for suspicious characters.

That meant good organization and tight control. Bob's thought turned to Hochner and instantly rejected him. Cunning, maybe, and capable of leading a holdup or a rustling, but no more. There was still another. Bob grunted at the hard implications of the thought. That man might be anywhere at this moment planning other depredations. Bob's badge would not be long on his shirt unless the unknown was found.

He jerked about when a soft knock sounded on the kitchen door. The room was almost completely dark. Balado had taught him to always keep his Colt near and it snugged in a holster and belt hung from his chair. He slipped the weapon from the holster as the knock sounded a second time. Bob crossed to the door and cautiously cracked it. He saw a tall figure in the darkness that he took to be a man until he recognized the long hair over wide, slender shoulders.

"Mrs. Richards!"

"Can I come in?"

"Wait until I strike a light."

He hurried to the table, heard her enter and close the door as he flamed the lamp. He turned to see her looking about the room. She wore a cheap dress of gray cotton. Her body, no longer hidden by jacket, shirt and Levi's, was breathtakingly feminine. Lamplight made her hair shine dark-red copper. He realized he stared, caught himself.

"Is something wrong, Mrs. Richards?"

"Going right well, thanks to you. Can't

complain of room or meal at the hotel." She looked at the table, at the cold range and the cupboards. "You've been riding all day, Sheriff, and I'd say you haven't had a bite to eat."

"I was just fixing to start supper. But what brought you?"

"First things first. Show me where things are and I'll get vittles started. We can talk while it's fixing."

"Now, see here! You'd best get back to the hotel. I can see you there — or my office — if something's wrong."

She gave him a patient smile and threw open the cupboard doors, surveying the food stock. She said over her shoulder, "Be obliged if you set the fire in the stove."

"Mrs. Richards!"

"You need something solid after all that riding. Where you keep your cold box?"

"It's over in that window." He pointed automatically, realized what he had done and snapped, "I'll not have you here."

"My, you're contrary, Sheriff! Near as bad as this morning. You settle down and have yourself another drink. Cooking is one thing I do know."

He blocked her progress to the cold box. "Mrs. Richards, this is my house. It's full night and I'm a bachelor and . . ."

"You're scared I'll bite you or something. The lamp's lit and this room is as far as I'm going. I'm going to fix your vittles and we'll do some talking. Then I'm going back to the hotel."

Again he saw that firm determination in lovely chin, jaw and mouth. Her sea-green eyes danced. "Besides, I might scream if you throw me out. That'd be worse, wouldn't it?"

She walked to the cold box, a crude arrangement of wire, burlap and dripping water that managed to keep food for a little time in this desert country. She paid no attention to Bob, who slowly sat down at the table.

Verda examined some meat closely by lamplight. Satisfied, she found beans and flour and coffee. Bob watched her, frowning, wondering how he could get her out. She seemed to catch his thoughts. "Figure it's easier for you to fire the range than to get me mad and yelling? Be obliged if you would."

He made the fire while she pounded and floured the steak. "My, lawmen eat good! Been a month or more since I've had chomp meat like this."

He glared at her back, then his gaze moved to her slender waist and the skirt that concealed her long legs. He growled, surprising himself, "If you're bound to be a nuisance, might as well cook for yourself, too."

"Now that's real thoughty!"

He made a disparaging, defeated sound and poured his drink. He watched her move with graceful ease from range to cupboard, to range again. As she made biscuit dough, Bob realized no woman since his mother back in Missouri had cooked for him.

Verda found a rough towel, brushed the flour from her hands and then worked over the range. She said, "You didn't have much luck hunting outlaws today."

"How do you know?"

"I was sitting on the hotel veranda when Tom Clayson rode in. Talk spread fast. Got to be more when Mort Jerris come in tuckered out and mad. Then you."

"I guess they would talk," Bob conceded. "But it's not every day you bring in an outlaw."

"Even a dead one."

Bob flushed at this allusion to her husband and snapped, "We've been over that."

"Right." She found the big iron skillet and greased it for the steak. "But today . . . town folks wonder if you're the gallihooting lawman they thought you were. You got to find yourself another outlaw — and that stage coach money would help a lot, too."

"I figure to find both."

The steak sizzled as she dropped it in the skillet. The aroma of cooking food filled the room and Bob's stomach felt empty and gnawing. Verda placed the big coffee pot on the stove and then came to the table, stood there and looked down at him.

"How you aim to find both?"

"I don't know . . . yet."

"Wish I could help you." She turned back to the stove. "But Sonora never told me much. Not that I wanted to hear after I knew what he was doing."

She said no more, as the final touches of the meal took all her attention. Then she came to the table and Bob looked on perfectly cooked steak, fluffy biscuits, aromatic coffee. She dropped into the chair across from him.

"Hope it's fitten."

For long moments both ate busily. She refilled his coffee twice, brought more biscuits and then served canned peaches. Finally Bob sighed contentedly. "You can sure cook, Mrs. Richards."

"I had the chance to learn," she said cryptically and started to gather up the dishes.

He checked her. "Leave 'em be. It's no more'n fair I take care of 'em. I want to talk to you."

"Not if it's to argue about me leaving Singara."

"No — not now, anyway. But why are you worried about me not catching an outlaw? Seems wrong, coming from you."

"You're thinking of Sonora. Friend, I never was nor will be of his breed of cat."

"You married him."

"Ever heard of a bad mistake?"

She read some of his unspoken skepticism. She flounced to her feet, strode to the stove and back with coffee for herself. Her eyes darkened as she looked into an unknown past. She stood wrapped in her thoughts, the table lamp bathing her in its soft light.

Bob felt the impact of her, the smooth oval of her face, the long, clean line of the nose and lips, harsh now but unable to conceal a sensuous inner fire. She took a deep breath and full, rounded breasts pressed against the cheap cloth of her dress. Bob's eyes dropped away. Beautiful, desirable . . . and trouble.

"You might as well know the story," she said harshly and dropped into her chair. "If Paw could've held onto that postage stamp spread of his in Texas . . . But we were pushed out by the big Flying W spread down there."

"We?" Bob asked.

"Paw, Maw and me. I was Verda Carr then. Anyhow, Paw was glad to take a penny on every dollar and get clean out of Texas into New Mexico. He'd work punching here and there, sort of grubbing, I reckon. We kept moving west to Benson, then down to Tombstone. Paw tried homesteading. Ike Clanton sort of encouraged Paw so he worked more for the Clantons than he did on his own ranch."

"Clantons." Bob said it like an ugly word.

"Being a lawman, you'd know of them. Paw kept herding more and more for 'em, both sides of the border. Paw brought in money. Maw and me had dresses and things for the shack — and food, too, I can tell you. Paw bought beef now and then when the Clantons gave him time."

She smoothed her hand over the table. "One day Paw rode out. Last we saw of him. Word come about a big robbery of a mule train just over the border near Nogales."

"I heard of that one. It was a massacre, too."

"I guess it was. Anyhow, just before then Sonoma Richards started to work for the Clantons. He come over first with Paw

95

about some kind of business. He kept riding over after that. I gave him no more welcome than politeness allowed, but he kept coming around. I thought I was rid of him when Maw and me moved to Tucson. That was when we knew for sure Paw wouldn't come back."

"Didn't the Clantons or Sonora tell you what had happened?"

"Not a word. Maybe didn't dare if it was them that robbed the mule train. Anyhow, Maw opened a boarding house in Tucson. That's where I learned to cook — morning, noon and night. And that's how I worked, too. So'd Maw, and for all our sweat and worrying, we just scraped by. Sonora'd come to Tucson every chance he'd get and board and room with us, sit around in the parlor. It was worse than before."

She suddenly pulled herself to the present and caught Bob's expression. She smiled, wry and hurt. "Just meals and sitting in the parlor . . . no more. Even if I'd liked him, I was too tired and too busy."

Bob flushed. She seemed to forget it on the instant. "Maw broke down under all the drudgery. She just couldn't get out of bed one morning and a week later she died. Happened Sonora was there and he stayed on. He sure helped during the time I had to care for Maw."

Bob watched her with a deeper understanding. Her head lowered and he saw the deep swirl of red hair falling down on either side of her face and over her shoulders. She made aimless tracery with a long finger.

"You can figure what happened. Maw dead and Paw gone. There was the boarding house but it just meant twice the drudgery it had before. Sonora had been kind. I sort of seen him differently right about then. Anyhow, I listened when he said we should get married. He wanted to come up here to Singara. He said he had a chance to make his way and with me to help him we'd get along real well. I was lonely, and mixed up and . . ."

Her voice faded off and after a moment Bob said, "You married him. I don't blame you."

"I do. I should'a known better," she flared. "Just three months before you come along, we heard about the fight between the Clantons and the Earps down in Tombstone."

"The OK Corral," Bob added.

"Sonora said he could've been in it and dead if he hadn't pulled out. He was outlaw rider for them and knew trouble was bound to come when the Earps took over the law. He just rode out while he had the chance

— and mostly on the money I had from selling the boarding house."

"Was he outlaw up here?"

"What else! In a month I knew I'd made the biggest mistake of my life. He was drunk most of the time. Then he'd ride off and be gone — a day, three days, a week. He'd show up like he'd just stepped out the door a minute before. He'd have money. But he went through it as well as mine. You should see the place where we lived!"

"I did. Today."

She looked up, green eyes searching. Then she shrugged. "Real comfortable place to settle down, ain't it? There I was, alone more'n half the time. I was figuring how I could pull out when Sonora tried for you but caught a bullet himself. Much as I hate to say it, you did me a kind of favor."

Bob shifted uncomfortably. "Do you know why he tried for me? He hunted me up in Phoenix first and then waited the next day in the hills."

"Two nights before he was here in Singara. I don't know why, or who he saw. The next morning he said he had to ride to Phoenix and he'd be back with a new dress for me and jingle money in his pockets."

"No idea who he saw here?"

"He never talked about what he was doing. Now and then riders would drop in but all strangers to me."

"Hochner?"

"Sonora was over there considerable. Curt came by now and then. Him and Sonora would talk private like. That's all I know."

"Would you know the strangers who rode in and out?"

"If I saw —"

A loud knock at the front door startled them. Verda jumped to her feet. The knocks sounded again. Bob slipped the Colt out of its holster again and stood up.

Verda said, "I'd better git."

She moved with flowing speed across the room. She opened the kitchen door and slipped out into the night. The door silently closed behind her.

The knocks sounded a third time.

IX

Bob swept up the lamp, paused for a glance at the door through which Verda had vanished, then strode down the hall to the front room and opened the door. Tom Clayson stood revealed in the lamplight.

He noted Bob's surprise and said dryly, "Now and then I do get away from El Ranchero, even when it's busy. I figured to talk to you."

"Come in. I was back in the kitchen having supper."

"Any coffee left?"

"There might be some."

Bob led the way, carrying the lamp. He placed it on the table and Clayson sat down. Bob lifted the coffee pot from the range and took a cup from the cupboard. As he turned, Clayson said, "I see you had company. Hope I didn't just barge in."

Bob almost told of Verda's visit, then thought better of it. "It's all right. Company left just before you came."

Clayson sipped his coffee at ease, but eyes constantly moving about the room, resting on the unwashed dishes that Verda had placed in a pan, the dying fire in the range.

Bob asked, "What's on your mind?"

"I figured you might be fretting about all of us losing trail today."

"I don't like it, of course, but I'm not fretting — at least not yet."

"Good enough. Don't."

"You've heard talk?"

"You always do." Clayson placed his cup on the table after slowly pushing Verda's to one side. "Thing is, we've never had a lawman before. Folks expect too much, especially when you rode in with Sonora Richards face down across his saddle."

"Luck — if you can call it that."

"But it happened. So some damn fools figure you should've come in today with all the outlaws and the Wells Fargo strongbox."

"I'm not a magician!"

"That's what I told 'em. My customers are important men in Singara and they listen to reason. They agree. What's more, they think you moved fast when the news came. They give you credit for it. Street talk means nothing when *my* customers back you — and they do."

"That's something, and thanks for helping me."

"No more'n I should since I was against hiring a lawman when the thing first come up to the county supervisors." He grinned at Bob's surprise. "That's right . . . and how wrong can a man think? You'd have heard about it sooner or later. It's no secret."

"That floors me," Bob admitted. "Mind telling me why?"

"It sounds crazy now, after I've met you and have sized you up. First, I was against it because it'd raise taxes, what with building the jail, buying and furnishing this house and paying your salary. Also, I figured the Federal Marshal could be called in if things kept on being bad — so no need for our own lawman."

"That's true enough."

"But short-sighted. Mort Jerris, Dick Rohlens and a few others showed me where I made a mistake. So I voted with them to bring you in. Now, I'm glad I did."

Clayson eased back in his chair and again his eyes moved to Verda's cup, to the stack of dishes across the room, back to Bob. "What you figure to do now?"

"Wait. Knowing the breed, I'm betting at least one of that bunch will spend money high wide and handsome in Singara, or in a neighboring county. The sheriffs will let me know and hold anyone until I can get over to question him. It's bound to happen. Tom, no matter how well they're organized or who their leader is."

"Now there I can't go along, Bob. Renegades get together for a job and then split up into lone wolfers just as they were before. Oh, you might pick up one or two of 'em, but you'll find there's no regular gang."

"We'll see."

They fell silent. Tom made aimless, circular moves with his cup and finally said, "What about that woman at the hotel?"

Bob checked a guilty start. "Still there, until I can figure what to do."

"If you don't mind my advice, get rid of

her tomorrow. There's a lot of talk getting over town. New, unmarried sheriff and a pretty woman like her are just asking for gossip — and getting it."

Verda's story flashed through Bob's mind, all of the trouble she had gone through and now malicious tongues promised to add more. He said tightly, "She'll be on her way somewhere soon enough, but right now she's down and out. What's wrong with helping her?"

"Nothing . . . only this morning you wanted to be rid of her pronto."

"Still do. But you just don't send her off to nowhere. Besides, she just might be the one to help us."

"Her? But she was married to an outlaw!"

"That's exactly why. For instance, she claims Sonora Richards talked to someone right here in town just before he rode out to ambush me."

"She's lying, I'd bet on it! If you had been here long enough, you'd know it, too."

Bob looked surprised at Clayson's vehemence. The man made an impatient gesture. "We have drifters in and out, and hardcases come and go, like every town. But none of 'em stay long. You know, I'll bet that woman is playing on your idea this is an organized gang. She can string you along by hinting she knows something — and she doesn't at all."

"But she just might."

Clayson reached for the bottle Bob had long before placed at the far end of the table. "Bob, you need a stiff drink to clear your head. I'd stake my future on the honesty of almost every man I know in Singara — and that's a lot of people."

"I'd still like to make sure," Bob said stubbornly. "I'd be a damned poor lawman if I didn't."

"All right, make sure. But in the next day or two. It's doubtful if you get a thing out of her." He lifted his glass. "Now . . . to Mort Jerris' money. May you bring it back to him."

"Amen to that!"

Clayson arose. "Take my advice, Bob. Don't let that woman string you along. She does you no good. The wives and ladies of Singara like a nice, moral sheriff who won't get tangled up with any woman, let alone a redheaded beauty once married to a renegade."

He saw Bob's jaw set and hurried on. "What do you think Mrs. Jerris or Mrs. Rohlens will say to their husbands? Or Madge Jerris to her father? Maybe we men have the vote, Bob, but it's the women of the town who have the real power. Don't get them against you."

He leaned over the table, hands grasping its edge to brace himself as he talked. He suddenly looked down at his hand. He held it out under the lamplight and Bob saw the long, coppery hair. Clayson looked knowingly at him.

"Good night, Bob. Don't let her make a damn fool of you."

Bob's face grew warm but Clayson had already turned, saying over his shoulder, "I'll go out the back way and cut directly to El Ranchero. See you in the morning."

Bob stood a long time in the doorway after Clayson's form had faded away into darkness. Finally Bob turned back into the kitchen. He poured a drink and stood with it in his hand, thoughts a'churn. The talk about Verda angered him and yet he must admit Clayson could be right. The next moment he knew Clayson was wrong. Lord! the girl had to have someone who would at least listen to her and give her a chance to prove herself.

But why was he so eager to be that person? He stared at the window that reflected the lamp, his tall figure and the kitchen behind him. He didn't know why he had come to so thoroughly believe in her. He could almost hear her husky voice telling him about herself. He could see her eyes, her moving lips, her slender body.

He hastily rejected the thoughts and feelings her image conjured up. He shook his head and spoke to his dark figure reflected in the window. "It's not that and you know it. It's just she was here and you got to talking. She's pretty and . . . you get that kind of hunger sometimes. That's all it is."

He picked up the lamp and walked to the bedroom to find the rest and sleep he so badly needed.

X

After a brief visit to his office the next morning, Bob walked to the Wells Fargo station. Three people waited for the westbound stage and out in the yard behind the building Bob heard men cursing and cajoling horses into place along the tongue of a huge freight wagon. The clang of a blacksmith's hammer added a steady, musical note.

Bob spoke to the clerk behind the counter and swung open the gate in the rail that divided the room. At that moment Mort Jerris swung around from his big pigeonhole desk, saw Bob and waved him into his office. "Morning, Bob. Close the door and sit down. What's on your mind?"

"Several things, like how much was in the strongbox and in what denominations?"

Mort handed him a slip of paper. "That's what Mason at the bank ordered out of San Francisco. Our home office will confirm Mason to the penny. As you see, goldbacks and greenbacks, gold coin, silver and copper."

Bob studied the slip and made a soundless whistle. "That's a lot of money to lose to outlaws."

"And we don't want to lose it. Wells Fargo will bring pressure on you if it's not recovered soon. They'll send, investigators and the Frisco bank will send Pinkertons."

"Tell me how a shipment like this works."

"A part of that was for the payroll at Hazleton's silver mine north of here and a part for the Golden Buzzard Mine payroll."

"But they *have* silver and gold!"

"Only dust and bullion, and keep little of that. Soon as they've smelted enough pure ore to fill a couple of saddle bags, fast riders race it into our bank here — generally at night and always by a different route. Mason gives 'em credit, ships the gold to the San Francisco mint by us — Wells Fargo. Mason in turn gets currency and coin shipped back to him. It's used by ranchers, miners and merchants to pay the help, buy equipment, cattle or merchandise, or it's loaned out by the bank itself."

"It's regular coming and going to San Francisco?"

"Not a regular schedule everyone knows about. We might ship or receive this week and again next — then it'll be a month, or five weeks. It might go out morning, afternoon or night by stage or in freight wagons carrying barrels of flour or cloth goods, so far as anyone knows. You can bet your bottom dollar we don't breathe a word about money shipments."

"Someone did about this one."

"No, the outlaws happened to hold up the stage that happened to be carrying it, that's all."

Here again came that strange disbelief that crime and outlaws might be organized in Singara. Bob sensed he wasted time in argument. "I guess they were lucky, looking at it that way. Did you expect the shipment?"

Jerris extended a telegram and Bob read, "Alice leaving for Aunt Emma's ranch. Thirty mile trip."

Jerris explained. "Thirty mile trip is code for expected date of arrival here. Too bad it was right on time or the bandits would've missed it."

"You told Mason, of course?"

"Of course."

"And I suppose he'd tell the mines and such?"

"Just those that had a right to know."

"And none of them would talk?"

"They'd be fools if they did."

A clerk interrupted them. "Word just come from Doc Laren, Mr. Jerris. That drummer who was shot has died."

"The shotgun guard?" Bob asked quickly.

"Nothing about Blaine, Sheriff. So I reckon he's still alive."

The clerk closed the door and Jerris shook his head. "Poor, unlucky devil!"

"But there are ten more unlucky devils. This is murder now. Somewhere, sometime, ten men are going to have ropes around their necks."

He stood up, aware of Jerris' shocked stare. "I'd best get along, Mort. I don't want your Wells Fargo boys spurring my flanks."

In the outer office, Jerris asked, "What are you going to do now?"

"Ask some questions first. I hope Blaine can talk. What I do after that depends on how much or how little I learn."

Jerris glanced toward the distant clerk and the waiting passengers. "That woman at the hotel, Bob . . . heard talk but didn't think much of it. Anyhow, what about her?"

Bob hid his flash of anger. "I bet you've heard! She's an outlaw's wife, Mort. I'm going to question her, too. She just might help us get your money back — and ten murderers. I reckon that would suit you?"

Jerris concealed embarrassment behind a fervent voice. "Nothing could be better!"

Madge Jerris came in from the street. She saw her father and Bob and she pushed through the gate before Bob could swing it open for her. She smiled, turned to her father, kissed him on the cheek and swung back to Bob.

"This awful thing, Sheriff! Mother and I talked about it just this morning. We're so glad you're in Singara."

"Thanks, but that doesn't mean much so far."

"Oh, but it does! We know you've done all you can and you'll do more. Mother and I are sure as sure."

She impulsively put her hand on his arm in a warm, electric touch and her eyes grew deep with concern. His mind registered the girl before him and Verda Richards in quick, confusing comparison. Mort looked at his daughter in surprised understanding, at Bob in swift appraisal, then back to his daughter.

Madge's fingers pressed Bob's arm.

"Don't you believe the doubters. Just don't believe them. Isn't that right, Daddy?"

"All of us are backing him, honey."

She smiled at Bob. "You see?"

"I reckon. Anyhow, you're making me feel better."

"I'm glad. Daddy, I think Sheriff James needs company. We'll have him for supper tonight. I'll tell Mother. You'll bring him home with you."

"But, Miss Jerris —"

"No buts, Mr. James. See that he comes, Daddy."

She left the office before Bob could make further protest. He looked around at Jerris, who shrugged. "She can sort of take charge, Bob. If you don't go home with me, I'll be in trouble. Nothing to prevent you, is there?"

He thought of the desert and the outlaw trails. It would be a lonesome job and perhaps a futile one. "I reckon not."

They made arrangements to meet at El Ranchero and Bob left the stage station. His eyes involuntarily moved to the hotel. He dismissed his vague, disturbing thoughts with an irritated grunt and turned toward the doctor's office.

Doc Laren confirmed the news about the drummer. "I figured the odds were way against him from the beginning. He's in the carpenter shop being fitted to a coffin if you want to see the body."

"No point. I'll send a wire to his company. See what they or his family want done."

"Just have to bury him, that's all. Nothing else to do in this weather."

"How about Blaine?"

"He'll pull through, being the tough jigger he is. He's over at his home so his wife can take care of him."

"Can I talk to him?"

"Sure. He'd like nothing better."

Half an hour later Bob sat beside Blaine's bed where the shotgun guard reclined, shoulder bandaged and arm in a sling. Now the leathery face had color and life and the eyes were alert and shrewd.

He cursed a twinge of pain under his breath and, at Bob's question, described the holdup to the point where an outlaw slug pitched hint out of the high coach seat and he lost consciousness.

"They took care of me first thing, Sheriff, seeing that, besides my Colt, I had the scattergun, and the rifle in the boot."

"Then you saw none of them?"

"Just a glimpse of a jasper popping up from behind a rock with a rifle at his shoulder. Bang! and I was knocked from the seat.

Funny how a small slug can hit you like a cannonball and —"

"So you saw no faces?"

"Just a bandanna. But that man stuck up like he was two feet away instead of sixty. Somehow I knew in a split second his rifle was aimed for me. You see things clear as clear then, and time goes slow . . . like me grabbing for my Colt, my hand reaching an inch at a time. Even saw the buttons on the jasper's shirt and the way he pulled the trigger."

"But that's —"

"His regular trigger finger was stiff, like it had been broken sometime back. It lay along the trigger guard and he used his second finger. You'd not think that'd make for straight shooting but I'm right here to prove it does."

Bob's eyes lighted, "A stiff finger!"

"Like this," Blaine illustrated.

Bob soon left the wounded man, feeling he knew at least one small identification of one of the bandits. He returned to the station just as the westbound coach pulled out with a shout and crack of whip. Bob moved through the settling dust to the big yard and asked for Hanlon, only to find the man loafed around town waiting to relieve the driver of the afternoon eastbound stage when it came in from Ehrenburg.

Bob finally found Hanlon at one of the lesser saloons, working over a solitaire layout. He looked up, kicked out the chair to his right. "Sit yourself, Sheriff. Heard about that drummer?"

"I did. And I talked to Blaine."

"He's coming along, thank God! Aim to get back on that lost trail, Sheriff?"

"I'm on it now." Bob smiled tightly at Hanlon's skeptical look. "There're more ways than one to trail owlhooters, friend — like getting a description."

"But I told you they was all masked!"

"So'd Blaine — and he saw only one before they got him. But he did notice *that* one had a stiff finger. Did you?"

Hanlon dropped back in his chair. He closed his eyes for a long moment. "Blaine's right. I complete forgot. The same jasper kept his gun on me while the rest went to work. He had his second finger on the trigger. First one was stiff and kinda crooked."

"So Blaine said. Know anyone around here like that?"

"Shucks, no! But, then, half the time I'm in Ehrenburg or down in Phoenix."

Bob stood up. "Thanks, anyway. Keep your eyes open for stiff trigger fingers — wherever you go."

114

He questioned the saloon owner in his office. The man had no memory that any of his customers had a deformed finger. "But, Sheriff, I don't serve 'em all. I got bartenders. We're all too damn busy to notice fingers."

"Will you after this? And let me know who the gent is?"

"Anything to help, Sheriff."

"Don't you or your bartenders let on I asked for this. Just come to me if you find the man and I'll do the rest."

He left the saloon and, on the porch, hesitated for a moment before he walked to the hotel with more assurance than he felt. Verda was not on the porch or in the lobby so he tapped the bell on the counter. The owner's wife appeared.

"Could you ask Mrs. Richards to come down?" Bob asked.

Mrs. Willets was short and rail-like, with a hatchet face and thin lips that finally curled disdainfully. "I take no messages to a woman like her."

"This is law business, Ma'am, and besides her way's paid."

"Indeed it is — by you. And what kind of law business is that!"

Bob glared but he fought for control, gained it. "I'll not argue, Ma'am. Just ask her to come down."

She stood rooted, scant black-clad shoulders pulled back in righteous disdain. "You can go get her yourself, Sheriff. She's in Room Five, as if you didn't know."

"Thank you. Want to chaperone us?"

"Indeed! Why should I?"

"So you'll have no reason to gossip."

"I don't gossip!"

"I'll make sure, Ma'am. I'm going to talk to Mrs. Richards out in the hall on law business. If another story gets around, I'll know where it started, won't I?"

He walked with deliberate heaviness up the stairs and along the corridor to the front of the building. Verda answered his knock so instantly he knew she had seen him from her window approaching the hotel. A glance beyond her confirmed the open window looking out over the flat roof and false front of the saddle shop across the street.

"Step out in the hall, Mrs. Richards?" he asked in a voice that carried back to the stairwell.

"Sure, Sheriff. That is, if this ain't a move to be rid of me."

"We'll talk about that later — soon. Please step out, Ma'am. You won't want it said a man was in your room."

"Not that they won't say it, anyhow, if I

know the women I've seen around town."

She swept by him a few paces, turned to face him. "Is this far enough?"

She wore last night's cheap cotton dress. She shook a wave of bronze hair back over her shoulder and stood proudly and angrily, vividly beautiful. "Now, what is it?"

"You said you saw some of your husband's friends. Did any of them have a stiff or twisted index finger?"

She thought long moments. "I don't remember none."

"Sure?" he asked and her nod sealed his disappointment. He suggested with faint hope, "Maybe you don't remember right now. If you do —"

"I'll tell you. That is, if you figure I got a right to stay in Singara."

There was an edge to her voice and her smile, but her eyes held something faintly like a plea.

XI

Bob returned to his office, hung his hat on a wall peg and dropped in the chair behind his desk. He folded his hands behind his head and stared blankly out the open door onto the street, empty of traffic in the noontime heat. His mind moved slowly over

117

the factors of his problem. He could ride out and follow the desert trails of the outlaws — seven that had not yet been traced. It was expected of him and he knew men asked one another why he did not.

But he also knew all of those trails would wipe out one way or another. So he would add failure to failure. A year from now the voters would remember the failures and Bob James would be out of a job.

But the alternative made him grimace. Its success rested on no more than his belief that the heart of the outlaw gang was here in Singara and the only slightly more tangible fact that a man had a twisted finger. Could he gamble that some of the stolen money would appear or that the finger would be spotted? Long, long chance — as easily dissipated as the vanishing desert trails.

His fingers absently touched the badge, traced its contour, felt the solid weight of it as he weighed the choice.

Thought of Verda intruded, bringing up another decision to be made. What was he to do with her? Should he send her off somewhere . . . if she would go? He heard her voice, ". . . if you figure I got a right to stay in Singara." She had the right, well enough, but it meant nothing without help.

Who's help? She looked to him, as proved by her outrageous demand.

In a way he should help because it had been his bullet . . . the old arguments battled across his brain. He saw Mrs. Willett's long nose and thin lips that could cast rumor and innuendo about the town. So, he dare not help Verda, for that would take the badge off his shirt as surely as incompetence in office.

Bob took a deep breath. Well, decision about Verda could wait until tomorrow or the day after. Maybe some solution would come. In faint surprise, he realized that while casting off that problem he had subconsciously come to a decision about the outlaws. He couldn't go against his own deep certainty that the key lay here in town. He would wait it out, watch for the mistake the smartest renegade always made. It would come.

Bob smacked his hands down on the chair arms and pulled himself up. He made his rounds of the town. The day slowly passed and, in late afternoon, Bob went home to bathe, shave and slick up for the evening with the Jerris'. He then walked to El Ranchero.

He saw a couple of ranchers deep in cattle talk at one table and Mason, the banker, and a mine owner at another. Two merchants stood at the bar who nodded friendly greeting as Bob came up. Clayson emerged from his office at the rear of the big room, saw Bob and came over.

Clayson waited until Bob had been served and the bartender moved away. "How's the sheriff getting along?"

"Tolerable, and no more."

"But busy, from what Doc tells me. Blaine help any?"

"Word gets around, don't it?"

"Small town. Besides, everyone's interested in what our new sheriff does." Clayson chuckled. "Even if Doc blabs a little now and then, he says you'll cut the mustard, give you time."

"I'm beginning to like Doc better."

"But Obed Willets at the hotel, on the other hand, don't think much of your tall redheaded woman. Thinks it's a disgrace."

"You mean his wife does."

"Obed never had a thought his wife didn't plant in his head. But what about Mrs. Richards?"

"She'll be a help, give her time. I'm sure of it now."

"She told you something about the outlaws today? Bob, like I said last night, she'll

say what she figures you want to hear and
—"

"Now you're beginning to sound like Mrs.
Willets yourself."

Clayson laughed, embarrassed. "I guess I
am a little, at that. But she does you no
good staying in town. Of course, if she tells
you the truth —"

"She's going to help," Bob cut in, hoping
to end the discussion. "I'll send her down
the road to wherever she wants to go in a
few days. But until then, I figure I know
what I'm doing. You said you had come
around to backing me and I've believed
you."

Clayson sobered and lightly touched
Bob's shoulder. "I still back you. Handle
the thing the way you see it."

Mort Jerris came in just then and Clayson
moved off as Jerris came up. He said, "We
have time for a drink before we go home.
Madge and the wife said not to keep supper
waiting. Let's go over to Mason's table."

The mine owner proved to be Hazleton.
He and Mason were filled with questions
about the progress Bob had made. Both
scoffed at the idea that the outlaws centered
here in Singara. Jerris looked at his watch.
"Gentlemen, me and the Sheriff have to get
along. Maybe we can argue this out later.

121

Anyhow, I know Bob won't let it drop."

Mason smiled. "I hope so, Mort . . . Sheriff. Can't let them get away with a haul like this, can we?"

Hazleton added, "I don't like to think of my money being squandered on drinks, women and such."

Jerris said stiffly, "It was in Wells Fargo care. You won't lose."

He gave Bob a quiet signal and they left the saloon. As they walked along the street, Jerris said grumpily, "You see how they figure, Bob. They sure want action. They'd like to have it day before yesterday. In time, my company will be asking the same questions. I don't want any part of your job."

Madge met them at the door and made them welcome. Her mother murmured polite words but Bob instantly sensed her withdrawal. Now and then she gave him covert, searching looks, not exactly filled with approval. Madge and her father kept the talk light, Mrs. Jerris occasionally adding a distant phrase or word. Bob was glad when they left the table. He and Mort had a drink while the women cleaned up the table. Soon Madge joined them with a regretful sigh.

"Mother has developed a terrible headache."

Bob instantly stood up. "I'd best go, then."

"Oh, no, Mr. James! It's not serious. She sends her apologies and asked I take her place. We can't have you leaving now, Mr. James. Daddy will look in on Mother while we talk."

She took his arm and turned him toward the door. "It's so nice out tonight. I think the swing would be pleasant."

They went out on the dark porch. They could look down the street on the shadowy houses and the dark land. Here and there golden rectangles marked lamplight in far windows. They said something to each other about the nice breeze and then fell silent.

As the swing moved back and forth, Madge sat with hands folded in her lap, head slightly lifted as she looked out into the darkness. Bob sought for something to say. She broke the long silence, asking about his life in Balado. He started hesitantly but soon warmed up under the spur of her interest. Now and then they swung into the lamp rays streaming through the window beside them and Bob became aware that her eyes held on him and her lips had slightly parted.

"So that's how it's been with me," he finished.

"It's wonderful!"

"No, it's a job, sometimes tiresome but now and then it gets rough."

"But . . . Sheriff! You're to the county what a mayor is to a city, or a governor to the Territory."

"That's what it's supposed to be but mostly it's just plain keeping the peace."

"It's a man's job," she stated firmly. Her eyes cut toward him and away again beyond the rail. "I bet your girl in Balado is proud of you."

"I have none . . . there or here."

"I see. But I'd never think of you with-out . . ."

Her voice died away. The swing moved slowly back and forth. He studied his hands, feeling a new constriction in his throat. He had heard the subtle note in her voice. He could say a few words that could lead to eventual courting. It would be easy to say them to the lovely girl beside him. His mind raced ahead to a vista opening before him. He could take her to church suppers, dances and such, come calling. Engaged or married to Madge, her father would sup-port him come next election. Maybe . . . he thought of Verda. Why did she intrude? She'd ridden into Singara and in a few days would ride out again.

"A girl would be nice," he said with a slow

groping. Madge didn't turn her head but her lips softened and her hand dropped onto the narrow space between them. "But there's no chance right now. I've got some owlhooters to catch up with. I've lost 'em so far —"

She turned, eyes alight and face determined. "But you'll get them, Mr. James. We all know you will. At least I do."

"I wish I could be sure. Wearing the law badge is a tricky business and a man can make bad mistakes."

"But you won't."

"Some think I already have."

They fell silent again. She absently toyed with the chain swing. "Maybe you have, but in another way."

"How's that?"

As they swung into the light again, he saw her embarrassment but also the set of her chin. She spoke with difficulty. "I hope you understand. I want to help you. I think you're just the sheriff we've needed and I don't like what people are saying."

"They expect me to ride out and —"

"It's not the outlaws, Mr. James. It's . . . well . . . understand *I* don't believe a word of the things I've heard. I'm sure a man like you — and a sheriff — would have a *good* reason to put the . . . outlaw woman up at the hotel. It's law business, I've told them, and nothing else."

He choked, "Well, thanks. I appreciate —"

She spoke gently but firmly. "I'm sure of it, Mr. James. But it would be wise if . . . well, she left town. My mother, for instance —"

"I noticed. But Mrs. Richards can tell me —"

Her hand dropped on his. "I know, I know. But you don't understand that people, especially old ladies, just love to talk. I've told them they're wrong."

She waited for his reply and her fingers, slightly tightened about his, drew away. He managed to choke out, amidst conflicting thoughts and emotions, "Thank you for trying to help, Miss Jerris."

"Maybe it's just meddling?"

"No . . . no, you're talking straight. It's well appreciated."

She stood up. "I should be getting in now."

"I'd best get back to Main Street and see if everything is quiet. Thank your mother for the supper. And thank you, Miss Jerris —"

"I'm Madge," she suggested softly.

She stood close and he started to lift his hands to her, caught himself and said thickly, "Thank you — Madge. Might be we could talk again sometime?"

"Yes, any time."

"Then . . . goodnight."

"Goodnight. And do think over what I've said."

Several yards down the dark street, he turned to look back just in time to see her walk into the house and close the door behind her. He knew she had been watching after him.

He walked slowly toward the main street. He knew, clear as day, he had only to say a word, make a move and he could count Madge Jerris as his. It was a stunning thought and yet he was angry with her. For that matter, he was angry with Clayson, all the whispering women, all the righteous who judged without knowing facts. Most of all, he was angry with Verda Richards and himself.

Main Street looked peaceful as he walked along it. He turned in at the first saloon, stepped just within the batwings. A glance at the dozen or so customers told him all was peaceful. The second place was a bit more crowded but just as peaceful. Yet as his sharp gaze swept the room, moving from face to face, over punchers and clerks, he suddenly wondered if some of the outlaws might be among them even now. No one apparently paid attention to him and he turned and walked out.

He came to El Ranchero and had no more than stepped inside when he saw Dick Rohlens signaling him from a corner table. Bob crossed the room and sat down beside the mayor. Rohlens asked, "How do things go?"

"All right. The town's quiet."

"Too quiet. Hear you've had supper at Mort's place. Maybe he told you we're wondering how you're moving against the outlaws."

"So do Clayson and Mason and Hazleton."

Rohlens signaled a waiter, indicated a glass for Bob. "Maybe we're too curious, not being used to the way lawmen work."

"Each works differently at different times, I've gone hell for leather riding when it was the thing to do."

The waiter brought the glass and Rohlens filled it for Bob out of his bottle on the table. "But it ain't the thing to do this time, seeing you're having a drink."

"Not yet, anyhow. Might be tomorrow — or the day after. I'm getting a line on who I'm going after."

"Folks wonder, though. About that and . . . Sonora Richards' widow. My wife heard something about that today."

Bob's cheeks flamed. "Two things about her you should know. First, I put her up over there instead of in a cell because she has no place to go. A hotel will cause less talk than me being alone with her in the jail during the short time she's here. Second, I think she can help spot some of the stage robbers."

"That part sounds reasonable."

"Then tell your wife so she can spread the word."

His acid tone made Rohlens look up sharply. "Now, look here —"

The flat crack of a rifle somewhere close in the night street cut him off. Every head in the bar lifted and eyes turned to the door. A second later the muffled scream of a woman jerked Bob to his feet.

He kicked over the chair as he whirled and raced toward the door. He was only dimly aware of Clayson's grim face and of the sudden, concerted rush of men behind him. He jumped out onto the porch; paused to adjust eyes to darkness.

He heard excited voices and saw dark figures racing toward the hotel. A strident woman's voice lifted in hysterical fear. "Help! They're shooting us!"

Bob plunged off the steps and across the street.

XII

He elbowed his way through the crowd about the hotel porch, raced up the steps and into the lobby. Mrs. Willets crouched at the far end of the counter, hands to her mouth, eyes tightly shut and face knotted in terror. Her husband, a frightened rail of a man, stood at the foot of the stairs looking up, his face pale. The cook, the waitress and some guests stood in a tight knot at the dining room door.

Bob jumped to Mr. Willets. "What's happened?"

"Upstairs. A shot through a front window. I heard her scream and then —"

Bob raced up the steps, slipping his Colt from its holster. He raced down the short hall to the front of the building. His shoulder struck the door of Room Five. Wood splintered as the inner bolt tore loose and he catapulted into the dark room. He felt a presence close by and something heavy made a deadly whispering sound as the blow just missed his head.

He spun about. He struck a soft body, heard stumbling steps and a thud. The low-burning distant hall lamp threw dim light through the open door. He glimpsed a crumpled figure, a petticoat and a long, shapely leg.

"Verda! You're all right?"

"Bob! Thank God! But . . . I nearly killed you."

He helped her to her feet. "What happened? You're not hurt?"

She stood close, looking at him with frightened eyes. His fingers felt the smooth, vibrant flesh of her bare arms and he became aware of white shoulders, a lifting curve of breasts beneath the coarse white cloth of her chemise. His hands dropped away and she whirled about, groping for her dress.

"I'm not hurt. Shot came right through the window and missed by an inch. I blew out the lamp and dropped to the floor." He heard a movement of cloth in the dark of the room. "Now I'm dressed."

Bob examined the window. It had been raised from the bottom so glass had not deflected the slug. He leaned out, aware of the growing crowd below, but his attention on the dark buildings across the street. The high false front and the low roof behind the saddle shop was directly in line with the window, offering shadowy concealment from both street and hotel.

He tried to pierce the darkness but it was difficult. The light streaming up from the hotel and El Ranchero below formed a blinding haze. He pulled himself back in. Verda asked, "Is he still there?"

"He'd be a fool if he was. He took a shot and then scooted." He pulled down window and shade. "Better light the lamp."

In a moment the steady yellow glow of the lamp filled the room. Her red hair made erratic waves of dark color over shoulders and back. Her dress had been hastily pulled on, buttoned awry. She stood in bare feet, her shoes at the foot of the bed. Her green eyes blazed in anger.

He saw a heavy piece of wood on the floor. Her gaze followed his, lifted in a mixture of fear and apology. "I tried to hit you with that. I didn't know. First the shot and then the door breaking open."

"I don't blame you." He picked up the improvised club. "Bed slat?"

"I guess. I just grabbed it and swung. I . . . might have killed you."

He placed the weapon against the wall. Then he saw the bullet hole beside the door and could trace the slug's path from the window. "Close. You took a chance blowing out the lamp. He could have fired a second.

You must've moved fast."

"I did. Not thinking — like trying to kill you. Bob, I'd never forgive myself."

"It's all right!"

Their eyes met and they fell silent. Something had happened in the last few swirling moments. Bob recalled the smoothness of her bare arms beneath his hands. It had been . . . "Bob — Verda" . . . and a fear for the other's safety. They silently questioned across the small distance between them but neither could answer.

Her gaze shifted away and he shuffled uneasily, said gruffly, "You can't stay here. You'll get another room. That jasper might try again."

Her head lifted and chin firmed. "Let me have a gun and we'll see how he tries."

"You'll have the gun, but —. Stay here until I come back. Leave the blind down and don't go near the window. You'll be safe enough for the time being."

He literally fled the room, not daring to remain with her. Out in the hall, the door now closed again between them, he stared at the ugly panels, still amazed and shaken by that long moment of silence.

He strode down the hall and stairs. The Willets headed a small knot of people standing at the base of the steps, curious faces lifted to Bob as he swiftly descended. Obed Willets asked, "Is everything all right up there?"

"Yes, other than a bullet hole in the wall."

"It was her — that woman?" Mrs. Willets asked sharply.

"Mrs. Richards — yes."

"She has to —"

Bob pushed by her and out onto the porch. Rohlens stood there and Clayson looked up from the street. Behind him stood half a hundred curious. Rohlens touched Bob's arm. "Anybody killed?"

"A try — that's all, Verda Richards. Not hurt."

He strode to the edge of the porch, looking down on the crowd. "You can go home. Nothing's happened. A damn fool got careless with his rifle."

They shuffled, growled and looked disgustedly at one another, then slowly moved away. Bob descended the steps, pushed through the disintegrating crowd and crossed the street.

At the rear of the saddle shop, he found a ladder leaning against the building. He looked up to the roof eaves, hand slowly rubbing the leather of his holster. Bob climbed the ladder onto the flat roof and walked quickly to the high false front, blackly outlined against the glow of lamps from the street below. He looked around one edge. He could see the whole front of the hotel, the few people still loitering around the steps. Directly on a line, he saw the dim glow of light behind the drawn shade of Verda's room and the sharp shadow of the lifted window frame. Bob drew back and struck a match. He caught a faint reflection of metal.

He picked up the object and held a new match flame close. He held a spent cartridge case, jacked out of a rifle chamber. The killer had prepared for another shot but Verda's quick act in blowing out the lamp had saved her.

Bob pocketed the case and retraced his way to the ladder. He thought he saw faint scuff marks but could not be sure. Not that it mattered. The ambusher had made good his escape and could even now be having a drink at a saloon, indistinguishable from anyone else.

Bob returned to the hotel. The Willets, husband and wife, met him in the lobby. The crowd had completely dispersed, even to the hotel help. Obed said, "Dick Rohlens wants to see you."

"I'll do that later. Right now, I want Mrs. Richards changed to another room, say facing the blank wall of a building."

"If she gets another room," Mrs. Willets cut in acidly, "it'll be somewhere else. She's moving — tonight."

"Mrs. Willets, someone shot at her and could try for her again, out in the street or in the room she's now in."

"No more than the hussy deserves. She's leaving this house right now."

"I won't allow it, Mrs. Willets."

She drew up, long nose twitching in anger. "You won't allow it? Indeed! Let me tell you this is our hotel and —"

"I'm sheriff." He tapped his badge and her eyes involuntarily followed the movement. "Mrs. Richards is important to the law. She's safer here than anywhere in town. So here she stays until this thing is over."

The woman's mouth hung open in stunned surprise. Then she caught her strident voice. "I don't care what she is. I *know* what she is. I don't care what you want. The law, indeed! I can see plain as plain you're stuck on —"

"Mrs. Willets!" Bob's thundering voice cut her short. "She stays, understand? You'll treat her like any other person. If you don't, I'll have you and your husband arrested for obstructing the law. I have to question that woman. I want her alive to answer. And I want her right here. Now — give me a key to another room."

The Willets stared at him. Then Obed wavered, turned to circle the counter and lifted a key from the peg board behind it. He handed it to Bob. Mrs. Willets turned in frozen, futile anger and dignity, and stalked out through the dining room.

Bob walked up the stairs, Obed staring after him. He tapped on Verda's door, identified himself and entered. She had smoothed her dress and brushed her hair, tying a narrow, white ribbon around it at the back of her neck. Bob told her what he had found on the roof across the street.

"You're lucky. But the point is, you're not safe." He jiggled the key. "You're moving to another room. Pack up."

"That's easy. You figure he'll try again?"

"I do."

She studied him a second, shrugged and pulled stuffed saddlebags from under the bed. "My shirt and Levi's. Boots right here." She pulled them from around the head of the bed. "I'm packed."

"Why . . . good Lord, you need clothes!"

"I told you how it was with Sonora."

He turned on his heel and led the way down the hall to a room toward the rear. He opened the door and moved across the room to the window. He lifted the blind and raised the window. About six feet away loomed the shadowy, unbroken wall of the general store. He peered at the dark roof above and knew that Verda could not be seen from there unless she stood directly within the window.

Satisfied, he pulled back into the room, struck a match and lit the lamp. Verda waited in the doorway and he said, "Come in. No view, but it's safe."

She dropped saddlebags on the bed. Bob pulled his Colt from the holster and dropped it beside the bags. "I reckon you can use it?"

"I'm from Texas."

"For once, I'm glad of it. If anyone knocks on the door, make dead certain you know who it is before you open."

He started to leave but she checked him. "Who wanted to kill me?"

"I don't know who, but I'm sure why. You know more than you've told me or than you know you know. We're having a talk tomorrow."

"I've told you everything!"

"There must be something you've forgotten. By tomorrow you might come up with something."

He waited in the hall until he heard the

key turned and the bolt shot into place. The lobby was deserted when he crossed it and stepped out on the dark porch. He looked along the street in either direction, eyes held here and there by the saloon lights. It looked peaceful and quiet but out there were outlaws and renegades posing as honest men. Somewhere, a killer who had failed waited for a second chance.

Bob's hand touched the empty holster. He hurried down the steps and toward his office for another gun. The unknown ambusher could as easily turn on him as on Verda.

XIII

The troubled faces of the men in the office belied the bright sun and mid-morning peace of the street. Bob had asked for the meeting, saying it would be best to talk to all the leaders of Singara at once rather than to explain to each individually.

Rohlens, Jerris and Clayson represented the town government and part of the county board of commissioners. County officials living miles away could not be present on such short notice but Bob mollified Clayson's uncertainty.

"It's unofficial, Tom. But there's been

enough wild guesses and talk that we should clear it up." He looked around at the other men. "You've heard about Verda Richards and that I put her up at the hotel. The ladies of the town are real upset about that."

Clayson said, "I'm part to blame for her being there — at least the first day. That's when Bob came to me for advice."

"What about last night, Bob?" Rohlens asked. "You sort of pushed your authority pretty far. My wife told me this morning and I checked with the Willets. They wanted to be shed of her last night and there's no law against that. But you —"

"— forced them to keep her and made them change her room," Bob finished. "Would you rather have found her dead out in the street?"

"Now that's a pretty big jump," Aronson, the saddler and a county commissioner, objected.

"Is it?" Bob pulled an empty cartridge case from his pocket. "I found this on your roof. Someone wants her dead."

Aronson's eyes rounded. "Now, I had nothing to do with it. I never knew —"

"Nothing," Bob agreed and placed the brass shell on the desk. "We're talking in circles, jumping here and there like wild broncs. Let's get the whole thing straight the way it happened. First, you began to have holdups, robberies and rustling in the town and county . . ."

He reviewed the chain of events from his hiring to the stage robbery and his own work in trying to find the bandits. He told of Verda's coming and of her demands. Here Clayson spoke up in ready confirmation. Bob told of her refusal to leave town.

"That was the whole problem at first," he concluded, "until I got my wits back and began to figure she had to know something since her own husband was one of the outlaws. So I've questioned her."

"And what did she tell you," Rohlens demanded.

"Damn little so far but —"

"Then get rid of her," Aronson said. "My wife's mighty upset that our own sheriff is fooling around. Them's her words," he added hastily.

"Now that brings up a point," Bob looked around at them. "None of you figure this ain't just a scattering of outlaws, getting together now and then to pull jobs like the stage robbery."

Jerris said, "Maybe I half believe that part, but I sure as hell can't think there's someone right in town heading them up."

The others made noises of confirmation.

Bob waited until the shuffling had subsided. "Then let's go back. Sonora Richards was sent to kill me before I could even show up in Singara and take the badge. His wife told me enough that I'm sure he had his orders from someone right here in Singara."

The men looked at one another as he continued. "And last night . . . why did someone try to shoot her? If she's just stringing me along, then why is someone afraid of her? Why use a rifle bullet to shut her up in case I question her?"

A long silence fell on the room, broken at last by Rohlens' petulant protest. "But you say she ain't told you a thing!"

"She's told me a little," Bob corrected. "Like she saw men come and go in that shack where she lived. She didn't know who they were or what they did, or why Sonora would be gone from time to time. But she must have seen faces and heard talk that didn't mean anything to her at the time. So she's forgotten it. I figure I can make her remember."

He looked around at them. "And that's what somebody don't want to happen. They'll try for her again."

"You mean to leave her in the hotel?" Rohlens demanded.

Bob pointed to the barred door behind

him. "I could move her into a cell but I'd have to be here day and night. How you figure the good ladies of Singara would take to that?"

"Oh, Lord!" Aronson breathed. "Let her stay where she is if it's that important."

"It is. Another thing — I've told the Willets her bill would be paid."

"Not out of your pocket," Clayson cut in. "The town and county can take care of that. What do you say — Dick? — Mort?"

Jerris nodded but added, "But when do we get on the trail of that stolen money?"

"Can't say when we'll get it, Mort," Bob answered. "But we will."

"Bob, before long we'll have Pinkertons behind every saguaro and palo verde if it ain't found. They'll figure you can't handle it."

The meeting broke up, the implication clear to all. None of them had demurred, and that meant city and county questioned its trust in Bob.

Clayson waited until the rest had left. "I keep figuring you wrong, Bob. Like this Mrs. Richards business and the way you handled this meeting. Did you know Rohlens was ready to call a showdown — get rid of the redhead or turn in your badge?"

"His dander's up that much?"

"Say his wife's — and Aronson's and Mort's. But you made us see it another way. I figure after that session we need a drink."

Bob opened a cupboard and set a bottle and glasses on the desk. The two men eased back in their chairs, drank, and then Bob poured a second that both of them nursed, each deep in his own thoughts.

Clayson said suddenly, "You know, Mrs. Richards is a good-looking woman and I know it as much as any man. But I figured you had — well, staked her out for yourself."

Bob wanted to pull away but didn't exactly know how. He said shortly, "No claim."

"Well, now! I just might get around to the hotel sometime. Since I know you have no personal interest, I just might see what happens before she leaves town."

Bob violently wanted to disagree. He remembered that potent moment of silence between Verda and himself. He heard Dick Rohlens' strong note of disapproval a few moments ago. He remembered Madge Jerris in the swing and her warning that also implied a promise on her part. Conflicting emotions held him tongue-tied.

Clayson turned to the window and looked toward the hotel. "I just might. Who knows? Nothing lost, anyway, is there?"

Bob managed a move of the head that could signify anything. Clayson turned from the window. "I'd best be getting back. You can't trust a bartender long."

He moved to the door and Bob said hastily, "I'll go up that way with you."

They walked along the street. Bob shot covert glances at Clayson, who strolled along seemingly unaware of the hotel. They passed it and Bob felt an easing of tension. A few yards further along, he said, "I'm turning in here, Tom. I need some rifle shells."

Clayson merely nodded, spoke a word and strolled on. Bob stepped into the General Store. Keeping an eye on the street, he bought two unneeded boxes of bullets. He returned to the street, looked toward El Ranchero. Clayson had disappeared. Bob felt relief and hurried to the hotel.

The lobby was empty and he mounted the stairs and knocked on Verda's door. She asked who it was and he identified himself. When she opened the door, he asked, "Can you come down on the porch? I figured you might remember something."

"Can't we talk here?" Then she smiled with a faint crook of her lips, "Oh, I forgot how it would be taken. Yes, I'll come down."

In a few moments they sat in rockers on

the porch, in plain view of the curious. There could be no possible whispers about this meeting, he thought, but then felt a touch of doubt that he hastily pushed out of his mind. "Have you remembered Sonora's friends?"

"There wasn't many, just drifting in and out, or now and then I'd see 'em over at Hochner's."

"The gent with the twisted finger?"

"I . . . ain't sure. Which finger was it and how did it look?" She watched closely as Bob illustrated how the man must have held and fired the rifle. She said slowly, "Just might be. But you'd never notice a finger like that if his hand was hanging natural."

Bob suggested hopefully, "But if he held a glass or a coffee mug, something like that?"

She thought and, slowly, her face lighted. "There was one. I remember now. He dropped by one day. Just drew rein and called the house. Sonora answered and a little later I went out to empty table scraps. He took off his hat and spoke polite. I remember now — he had a stiff, twisted finger and it stuck up funny when he held his hat."

"Who was he?"

"I don't know. He rode off. Sonora said the man rode for Hochner now and then.

Sonora never said his name." She saw his disappointment. "I'm sure sorry but, honest, that's how it was."

"You'd know the man if you saw him again?"

"Yes, but I never have."

"You just might, if I find him." He stood up. "I've told the city officials about you and how you've helped. They say you're to stay here a while, figuring we might need you."

She also stood up. "Ain't that nice of them! And afterwards?"

"We'll see. 'Bout all I can say now."

She studied him and he felt the impact of her eyes, sensed a softening that disturbed and puzzled him. "I guess I can't ask for more. Not now, anyhow."

He flushed, turned his hat in his hand, wondering how to relieve the sudden tension that had come between them. Avoiding her eyes, his roaming glance fell on El Ranchero and he blurted, "Someone has an interest in you."

Her face lighted. "I wondered — !"

"Tom Clayson. Runs El Ranchero." Her expression changed to disappointment. "He said he might call on you."

"He did? Do *you* mind?"

"I — well —" He met her eyes, again soft

147

and searching. "Well — what have I to say about it? There's nothing —"

He turned on his heel and hurried away, jamming his hat on his head. He almost raced across the street. He finally surrendered to the impulse and looked back. He saw Verda just disappearing within the hotel doorway.

He stopped at the stage station, a corner of which was the town post office. He had a small stack of reward dodgers, nothing more. He moved to the canopied porch, dropped on a bench where travelers waited for the stage. He could see El Ranchero just across the street and, a short distance beyond, the hotel. He forced them both out of his mind and examined the reward dodgers. Now and then he would look up, half expecting to see Clayson walking to the hotel.

Bob abruptly asked himself what he thought he was doing! Here he sat as though waiting for a stage that would not come for many hours. He read dodgers scrupulously but could hardly remember a word. He watched the saloon and the hotel.

He mentally asked, "How come you're just sitting here, fooling yourself? You're watching to see what Tom does about Verda and you can't argue it any other way. Suppose he did walk right down there and meet her? What could you do about it? And what does it matter?"

He calmly refolded the dodgers, and stuffed them in his hip pocket as he stood up. He walked toward his office, passing the saloon and the hotel, rigidly keeping his eyes straight ahead. When he rounded the turn, he felt a small sense of triumph. His stride slackened as he continued to his office.

He dropped the dodgers on the desk and eased into the chair behind it. He tried to think of what Verda had unknowingly hinted about Hochner and told him about the man with the stiff finger, but her vision kept interfering, or he'd imagine Clayson walking confidently to the hotel. He heard Tom's voice, "I just might see what happens."

He shifted edgily and tried to bring his thoughts back to a focus. They refused, though he tried again and again. The crooked finger, Hochner, Verda and Clayson moved in meaningless succession. He grunted angrily, looked up at the wall clock and stood up with a new decision. He lifted a rifle from the rack and took a box of shells from the desk drawer. He loaded the weapon then checked his cartridge belt and Colt. Carrying the rifle, now in a scabbard, he went outside and circled the building to

149

the corral.

A few moments later, he rode to his house. Ten minutes later, he emerged with saddle roll and canteen; binoculars in a case. He strapped them to the saddle and mounted. He rode toward the hotel. No one was in sight when he rode by. As he approached El Ranchero, Dick Rohlens came out, saw him and signaled him over.

The mayor eyed the rifle in the scabbard, the cased binoculars and the full cartridge belt about Bob's waist. "Looks like you're hunting for bear."

"Hope it works out that way."

"Where?"

Bob indicated the hotel. "She gave me a new idea, Dick. Kind of thin but worth following. Still, I don't reckon I'd better talk too much right now."

"I'm the mayor," Rohlens suggested.

"Sure — and county commissioner. But if the law tells who it suspicions, everyone begins to have ideas." He looked steadily at Rohlens. "Ideas they don't forget even after the law might say it made a mistake. Suppose I checked you, or Tom or Mort?"

"I savvy."

Bob looked beyond him at El Ranchero. "Tom's busy?"

"Working on his books."

Bob touched finger to his hat brim. "Well, I'll let you know, bull's-eye or miss."

A few moments later, he turned into the Prescott road. The last Mexican adobes wheeled behind him and he faced the open road and the small, rolling hills. Free of the town, he suddenly felt free of turmoil. He took a deep breath and looked far ahead down the road. He was lawman now, and nothing else. It felt good.

XIV

Long before he came to the Hochner ranch, Bob left the road and allowed the horse to set its own pace across the semi-arid land. He rode at an easy slouch but his eyes constantly moved from one barren, sandy ridge to another. When he judged he was close to the spread he sought, he dismounted and cautiously climbed a low slope. He had to do this four times before he finally looked down on the scabrous ranch.

He saw only a single horse in the corral. Nothing moved in the ranch yard but quivering heat waves that distorted everything. He dropped back below the rim of the ridge and surveyed the desolate country about. He rode west for some distance and dismounted behind another low ridge. He ground-tied the horse and cautiously approached the low crest. He now viewed Hochner's ranch from another angle and a greater distance. Using the binoculars, he could pull the house almost up to his nose. Satisfied, he eased to comfortable position and set himself to the vigil.

Nearly an hour later, he saw a rider come slowly to the ranch from the west. Bob watched until the man rode into the corral and then put the glasses on him as he dismounted. Hochner appeared in the doorway, said something and stepped back inside.

The rider whom Bob's glasses brought up close proved to be Jowett. Bob lowered the glasses and watched the distance-dwarfed figure leave the corral and go into the house. Bob settled himself to wait and watch. The sun dropped behind the western mountains. Light lingered, slowly waning. A single star appeared and Bob began to think of cold-camping in some hidden spot for the night. Then two riders appeared along the trail that branched off the main north-south road miles away.

Bob trained his glasses on them. They came in sharp focus as they approached the house. Hochner stepped out, Jowett just behind him. All four came into clear, close view through the binoculars. The two newcomers were strangers, though Bob had the feeling he had seen one around the Singara saloons. The four talked a moment, then the newcomers, leaving their horses ground-tied, followed Hochner and Jowett into the house.

A light glowed from a window. Bob replaced the glasses and studied the waning light, checking impatience. There was no way to slip up to the adobe with any chance of concealment. The day faded with torturing slowness but, at last, Bob felt he could move unseen. He quickly topped the ridge and dropped down its far slope. Now even nearby sentinel-like saguaro were no more than ghostly shadows. The lamplight from the adobe glowed strongly but the building itself had disappeared into darkness.

He made a wide circle while yet some distance out to put the building between himself and the horses. Then he moved in. Gradually the adobe began to shape up as a darker shadow and then a black outline against the starlight. He eased along its wall to the corner, slowly edged around it. He sharply eyed the saddled horses several yards out but they made no sound. He moved carefully toward the rectangle of streaming, golden light marking the window.

He was still several feet away when he heard muffled voices and then a startling burst of rough laughter. He realized the window was open to the warm desert night. He gave mental thanks to the gods of lawmen as he moved slowly to the window and pressed against the adobe wall beside it. He heard, in mid-sentence, a voice he thought to be Hochner's, ". . . and that's where you catch him."

"He'll not expect trouble there," a second voice approved.

"That's right. If you pull it slick, there won't be any shooting. We've had enough of that. The drummer died and that means murder. The damn' fools —"

"Aw, Curt! Joe had to do it. The drummer pulled a derringer and — what would you do?"

"Forget it. Let's get back to the job. You shouldn't have no trouble. Joe will meet you near the arroyo. Turn the stuff over to him and he'll ride to the Notch. Like always, you'll get your share in a week."

A third voice asked, "You're damn sure that's the route he'll take? Otherwise, we could be sitting out there for a month."

Hochner's heavy voice filled with contempt. "Now when has the Brain or me ever

154

missed?"

After a second's silence, the complainer said, "You're right, Curt. Let's have a drink on it."

Bob heard only small sounds, no voices. He wished he could chance a look through the window but dismissed the thought. His binoculars had already revealed the men inside. A voice suddenly said, "Sonora's wife worries me. The redheaded wench might let something drop."

"Her and that sheriff have sure been pow-wowing," a second voice added.

Hochner said, "You tend to *your* jobs. She ain't one of 'em."

"I'da done a better job of shooting, any-how. Right across the street and a clean miss!"

"Time'll soon come again," Hochner growled. "And you can bet — no miss."

"Sonora did — and now we got a sheriff nosing around."

"Not for long," Hochner chuckled grimly. He spoke in warning. "You two'd best hit leather so you can be all set to meet your friend."

Bob began to edge back to the corner but had taken no more than two steps when the door flew open and a wide band of light streamed across the sandy yard to the saddled horses. Bob dropped in a crouch low against the base of the building, hardly out of the full reach of the light from the door. He held his Colt with hammer back and ready. His breathing grew shallow and every muscle tensed.

The two riders came out. Hochner appeared just within the doorway. A single glance in Bob's direction by any one of the three would disclose his presence even though he partially merged into the shadows. He held himself unmoving, head slightly lowered so that the black, wide brim of his hat would hide his face.

The two men walked to their horses, picked up the dangling reins. Hochner called a warning, "Now don't miss connection. And no killing."

The men swung into saddle. Now they faced the house but their attention held on Hochner, silhouetted in the lamplight behind him. "Depend on it, Curt. Where do we get our divvy?"

"I'll let you know. But it'll be in a week."

One of the riders waved a hand and both reined about and rode slowly off into the night. Hochner remained in the doorway. Bob heard Jowett, inside the adobe say, "They'll be all right, Curt."

"They'd better be! The Brain didn't like

what happened to that drummer and he's
—"

Hochner turned inside and closed the door. Bob eased out his breath in a long, soft sigh then moved slowly back along the wall to the corner. That gained without alarm, he moved with increasing speed toward the distant low ridge and his horse.

A short time later, he topped a dark ridge and looked back at the small yellow light in Hochner's adobe then around at the great sweep of darkness that hid the whole of the desert country. Two men rode somewhere out there and Bob knew he now had no chance to follow them. Nor did he want to chance an encounter with Hochner this close to the adobe come daylight.

He moved down the ridge to his horse, mounted and moved slowly eastward. He busily thought over what he had learned. A robbery was planned, that he knew. But he had no idea where or against whom. There was nothing he could do to prevent it, the two riders having vanished in the night. But now he had definite confirmation that he had been right from the beginning. The Brain, the leader — so Singara's crime and outlaws were all one band, striking where directed. Who was the Brain? And where?

Bob's fist struck the saddle horn. "Singara! Has to be. It's the center of the county and that's where the jasper is."

Then he thought of Joe and smiled grimly. He knew Joe was the man with the twisted finger. A common name, true enough, but not likely two of them in one band. The first lights of Singara began to twinkle far ahead and he touched spurs lightly to pick up his pace.

The first houses crouched dark and sleeping but the lights from the saloons glowed and a shaft streamed out a window of the stage station. His first glance at El Ranchero recalled the situation with Verda and Clayson in full force. He swerved to the hitchrack and dismounted.

The place was nearly deserted. At first he saw only the bartender then two ranchers in deep conversation at a far table. He felt a shock at the thought Clayson was gone . . . to the hotel? Just then Clayson came out of his office, saw Bob and came over. "I heard you'd ridden out."

"No one misses a thing in this town!"

"Nothing. You learn to live with it. Find anything?"

"Desert, mostly."

"We're all hoping you'll get that money back."

"So am I — and I will."

"Have a drink on it." Clayson signaled his bartender. He yawned. "It's been a long day. Didn't step a foot outside all day."

Bob accepted the drink, wondering why he felt such relief. A subtle barrier between him and Clayson vanished. They exchanged a few words and then Bob left. Out on the porch, he decided to make a round of the saloons before turning in for the night. Two of them wound up the day's business and, as he approached the third, the lamplight snuffed out, the owner and bartender emerging on the dark porch.

"Hey, Sheriff," the owner called. "You're out late."

Bob strolled with them to the stage station where they parted. Bob stepped up on the porch and tried to open the door. It was locked, though lamps glowed in the waiting room. The rattle of the door knob in Bob's hand sounded loud and a second later Jerris peered out the door of his private office. He admitted Bob. "Find something?"

"Nothing to talk about. What keeps you 'til this hour?"

"Book work and monthly report."

"Sorry I broke in."

"Don't be. I feel safer knowing you're patrolling the town. So does everyone else. Only thing . . ."

"Why don't I bring in a bunch of bandits?"

"Something like that."

"I reckon folks will have to wait. Goodnight." He turned to the door, checked. "Ever heard of something called the Notch?"

"Not in years. A gold strike petered out there maybe ten years ago. Boomed enough in a month to have a shack town. Abandoned now. Maybe thirty-forty miles northeast. There's still an old road — trail now, if it's there at all — cut through the Rattlesnake Hills. They called the cut the Notch."

"Not used now?"

"Oh, a small cattle drive comes that way, but not often. How'd you come to hear of it?"

"Someone mentioned it and I wondered what it was. Good night."

Jerris yawned and said good night himself. He locked the door behind Bob and walked wearily back to his office. As Bob rode by the hotel, he gave its dark facade a long, searching look. Only a low-trimmed lamp gave dim illumination to the lobby. He rode on to his office, took care of his horse and trudged wearily home. He fell into bed.

He awakened refreshed in the morning, mind clear. As he ate his breakfast, he reviewed what he had learned crouched below Hochner's window. He sat over a final coffee, eyes narrowed as he visioned the far distances of desert beyond the town. A robbery could happen anywhere and to anybody. He could only let it happen. This was always the odds against the law. A crime must first be committed.

But he did not have to wait here for news of the holdup. He knew it would happen and he also knew delivery of the loot would be made to "Joe" at the Notch. That was the place to be. Both swag and Joe would fall into his hands and he had already seen the faces of the robbers-to-be.

He stood up, swung his gunbelt about his lean hips. A lawman seldom had such a streak of luck. If he played it right . . .

He hurried to the office, picked up rifle and binoculars and saddled up. He rode to the hotel. He found Verda in the dining room and sat down at her table despite the frowning disapproval of Mrs. Willets.

Verda said, "I hoped you'd be back."

He had to study his hands to conceal the sudden warmth that surged through him and fought to keep his voice low and level. "I can't stay long. Has there been any trouble? Noticed anyone watching you?"

"No trouble — and no watchers. Oh, and no . . . Mr. Clayson."

161

He looked up with a pleased grin that he immediately checked. "Sure relieved about it all. But that don't mean they won't try again. Keep close to your room and the hotel."

He shot a sidelong glance at Mrs. Willets, who frowned from the kitchen doorway. Just then two drummers came in and their noise covered Bob's low voice. "Did you ever hear of the Brain?"

"Yes," Verda answered instantly. "Now and then Sonora would say something about him."

"Did he say who he is?"

"No . . . just the Brain. That time he came back to say he had a job — you — he said the Brain ordered it."

"Here in Singara?"

"Had to be. But I don't know who the Brain is."

Bob's eyes sharpened with new alarm. "But he sure knows about you. That's why someone tried for you. Now you keep close. Hear?"

She nodded, sensing his urgency. "You'll be close by, won't you?"

"Tonight or tomorrow at the latest. But everyone will know I'm riding out, the Brain among them. He might figure it'd be good time to try again."

She flashed him her vivid smile. "You ride easy. You left me a gun."

"Use it pronto if you have to."

He left her at the table. As he emerged from the hotel and hurried down the steps, a woman's voice called, "Sheriff James!"

He turned to face Madge Jerris. She looked slim and lovely, a parasol shading her from the morning sun. But Bob noticed something hard in her violet eyes and a harsh set to her lips. But her voice, soft and musical, belied eyes and mouth. "Good morning, Sheriff. About early, I see."

"Law business, Miss Jerris."

Her glance at the hotel was silent accusation and challenge. Her tone grew faintly acid. "I suppose you're getting more information from — Mrs. Richards? Important, I imagine."

"Yes it is. Now I've got to ride."

Her gaze moved to his horse, rested on the rifle in its scabbard, then turned to him with new uncertainty. Suddenly he understood her warring thoughts and read the decision a split second before she spoke.

"Of course, Sheriff. Whatever *she* says."

XV

It wasn't until he had turned into the Prescott road that he felt the full impact of Madge Jerris' last comment, the contempt in it for himself as well as for Verda. She had judged and rejected him once and for all.

There'd never be anything between him and Madge Jerris now, even if Verda Richards left town today. Even more, he could count on the girl's dislike, if not hatred. She'd fully side with her mother, with Mrs. Willets, with the other women. That would bring pressures on Dick Rohlens, Mort Jerris and all those men who could fire Bob as easily as they had hired him.

He thought that somewhere ahead he'd find the Notch and, if luck held, Joe and the stolen loot. Bob would return to Singara as triumphantly as he had first entered. With Joe a prisoner, the Brain would have a real name, a face, and could be arrested. There would be no further need for Verda Richards. This ride, Bob told himself, would solve all his problems.

So he dismissed it all and set himself to the journey. He came out of the low hills and, far ahead, hardly more than a faint blue line, rose the high mountains, the end of the desert country. He watched for a trail or an abandoned road that would lead off to the northeast.

Miles rolled by but he doggedly rode on. More miles, and now he could see the mountains more clearly, a rugged, rocky rampart blocking the northward spread of the desert.

Then he saw the road just ahead. It was almost obliterated, but the freighters and coaches that had served the boom camp had left a mark that time and the desert sands and winds could not wholly erase. It was like a ghost of a thoroughfare. He turned into it and soon the Prescott road disappeared behind him.

The mountains grew higher and higher as he approached them. The ancient trail he followed threatened to vanish altogether but never quite did. Once he saw an ancient cutting of iron wagon tires, a trace only a foot or two long, preserved all these years at the base of a clump of ocotillo. A casual glance would have missed it.

The desert floor began a slow lift to the nearing mountains. Bob could see only ramparts of sun-drenched rock, broken faces of cliffs, a solid wall except for one dark opening that marked a canyon. Even from this distance, it looked too wide to be called a notch.

He finally approached this wide natural cut in the cliffs and drew rein. Recently churned ground marked the path of a cattle herd passing this way. The sign angled off westward toward the distant Prescott road. Jerris had said the old trail was occasionally used and this was proof — maybe two or three months ago, Bob judged.

He turned to the canyon, feeling he must be nearing the Notch. He looked for fresh sign of a single rider coming up this way but found only the aging cattle trail. Still, he jacked a cartridge in his rifle chamber as he searched the high, jagged rim above. Only rock broke the skyline.

Bob rode on, alert to the canyon ahead and what might lie behind the next turn. The canyon opened and Bob found himself looking down into a long and narrow valley. The ancient traces of the road descended the short slope and the old cattle tracks were clear. Across the valley, another canyon led deeper into this wild tangle of barren rock.

Bob set the horse to the slope, giving the outlaws credit for picking such an area in which to pass along stolen loot or to hide should the occasion warrant. He pulled his hat brim lower against the blinding sun. The second canyon began to narrow as its floor gently lifted, indicating that Bob approached the higher mountains beyond. He rounded several turns, made yet another and instantly drew rein.

Straight ahead, the canyon walls pinched in, so high that the sun now could not touch the rocky floor. Just beyond the canyon mouth a high sliver of barren rock, so placed that it divided the canyon, stood black and tall. It was as though the canyon floor was a straight rifle barrel and the rock the front sight — all gigantic.

This could be nothing but the Notch. Bob's hand dropped to his holster as he slowly searched canyon mouth, rock, and then the walls to either side. Nothing moved. Still, he tested the silence with a sixth sense developed long ago in Balado.

He moved slowly toward the canyon mouth. He reined in just before leaving the protection of the canyon. Now the rock in the shape of a rifle sight loomed just ahead, actually on the down slope. It stood fifty feet high, worn by wind and sand to a sharp, high ridge. Bob looked beyond it onto a wide valley and saw, perhaps a mile out, the crumbling shacks of what had once been a town.

Bob slowly rode clear of the canyon. His

eyes darted left and right along the walls of the cliffs to either side. There were many great rock pockets in which a rider could hide. But no one challenged. He looked down at the ground but saw no more than the old cattle tracks. No rider had come this way.

Bob looked back along the canyon the way he had come. He studied the slope, the valley, the distant ghost town, then the cliff walls the length of the valley to either side. He searched the cliff face, nearly two miles away across the valley, with binoculars; held them on a canyon for a moment and then moved on.

This was the place where someone would take the loot that Joe had received from the actual robbers. But from what direction would Joe come? Or the man he was to meet? The canyon back of him? Across the valley before him? Or along it from either side? Bob lifted his hat and swiped wrist across sweating forehead as he considered the problem. Any choice could prove deadly wrong.

He again studied the natural alcoves formed by the broken cliff faces, some shallow and some deep. They offered the only concealment but, even so, would not be too good if his man approached up the slope out of the valley. He turned his horse right. The third depression proved deep enough to conceal both himself and his mount. He dismounted and ground-tied his horse close to the rear wall. He returned to the alcove's mouth and looked toward the canyon.

It was within easy revolver range. Bob moved back out of sight of the canyon and studied the slope below him. If his man came out of the canyon and rode toward the ghost town, Bob would see him within three horse lengths. Bob returned to his horse, took canteen, binoculars and rifle and found a spot just within the mouth and sat down to wait, back against the rocks.

At first he watched the slope and the valley. Twice he scanned the distant ghost town with the binoculars, seeing only broken windows, gaping doors, crumbling adobe and sagging roofs. Satisfied it was deserted, he forced himself to patience.

The sun moved across the sky in a steady arc. Bob's thoughts wandered lazily as he felt enveloped in the great silence of the desert. He wondered what the ghost town had been in the days of its boom. He could imagine — eager men, a few canny merchants, gamblers and girls. Their little shacks would stand in a row over there somewhere, hidden by the larger buildings.

There'd be saloons — plenty of them.

Suddenly he thought of the saloons of Singara, El Ranchero in particular. He saw Tom Clayson, young and handsome, as Bob believed Verda Richards would see him. Would Tom have gone to the hotel by now? Would he and Verda be talking? The picture of Tom smiling into Verda's sea-green eyes and receiving her smile in return brought a thickness to his chest.

He tried to blot out the picture but failed. He wanted to be in Singara — right now, this minute. He shouldn't be miles away while Clayson soft-talked her! Why, it might have gone even further by now!

He took a deep breath and stared in sheer amazement out over the empty valley below. Why . . . damn it! He was jealous of Tom — or anyone. Why?

"Good Lord!" he said aloud to the desert air. He must be in love with her! He shook his head but then he knew he could not deny it. When? How? The night the ambusher . . . ? No, before that. When?

A faint sound in the direction of the canyon cut off his bewildering thoughts. He came to his feet in a silent flow of muscles as a man rode into sight out of the canyon. Bob saw a stocky figure, broad back and wide-brimmed hat as the man searched the valley below. Bob saw the glint of cartridges in the looped belt, bulge of holstered gun and heavy saddlebags behind the saddle, another pair before it.

Bob ducked back as the man's head swivelled his way. He heard an impatient stamp of a hoof and a low curse of disappointment. Hooves sounded again, slowly growing louder and Bob pressed against the rock of the cliff. He saw the distorted shadow on the ground before the rider came into view.

"Joe!" Bob called softly.

The man's head turned, momentary expectation showing on a beefy, bearded face. He had ugly, moist red lips beneath a beard. His eyes widened in stunned surprise as they rested on the sheriff's star. Without warning, his hand slashed to his gun. The desert silence shattered in a double roar of Colts. Rock chips flew by Bob's chest and a fragment bit at his cheek.

The man in the saddle fell away from Bob, his gun glinting as it dropped to the ground. His horse snorted, shied. Bob jumped to grab its bridle. The falling man's boot had twisted in the stirrup and he hung head down, arms dragging the ground. Bob's slug had caught him high in the chest, just below the neck. The massive body shuddered and went limp.

Bob calmed the horse, freed the caught boot and the body tumbled on itself like a sack, right arm flinging out like a puppet's. All but one finger was curled. It stood straight and stiff, twisted. Bob had found Joe — and killed him.

The outlaw's horse skittered but Bob held it in. Then he ground-tied it and examined the saddle bags. Those before the saddle held rations and extra bullets for the Winchester resting in a scabbard.

But the bulging bags behind the cantle held gold bullion in small bars. The insignia of one of the mines had been stamped in the soft yellow metal of the bars as identification. Bob whistled soundlessly.

The bandits had hit a gold rider and now Bob understood why they worried about missing. The mines shaped their gold into small bars to send to town for shipping to mints. A fast, well-armed rider carried them. He never left the mines on a regular schedule or rode the same route twice. He could ride at any time — high noon, midnight or any hour in between. Bob thoughtfully restrapped the bags. The outlaws had known exactly when and where to wait. This meant that the mine manager, his assistant, or Mort Jerris at Wells Fargo — the only three to know — had let the information drop to someone they knew and trusted. That someone could only be the Brain.

Bob looked down at the dead outlaw. There lay the man who would have been able to identify the Brain. There lay one of the stage coach robbers who could have identified his companions and told what had happened to the loot. But now he never would.

Bob silently cursed the bad luck that had made Joe try gunplay. But his mind fastened on the fact that Joe had come to the Notch to turn the bullion over to someone. Bob bent to the body and his muscles bunched as he worked the dead weight into position to tie it across the saddle. He swiped forearm across his forehead, fingered sweat from his eyes and then led the horse into concealment beside his own. He returned to his former place to wait.

Less than half an hour passed when a moving object down in the valley and far over to his right caught his attention. He made it out to be a single rider. Bob considered the distant rider a long moment, then looked back over his shoulder at Joe dangling limply across a saddle and then down in the valley again. Let challenge come up here and the dead body behind him be a complete surprise. He waited.

The newcomer rode directly for the mouth of the canyon. The sounds grew louder and Bob picked up the reins of Joe's horse. Leading the animal, he spurred his own horse forward. When he rode out, the newcomer had drawn rein in the canyon mouth. The sound of the horses made the man swivel around in the saddle and Bob looked at Curt Hochner.

Hochner's beefy face grew slack in shock as his eyes cut to the dead body and then back to Bob.

"Know him, Hochner? I hear he was called Joe."

XVI

Hochner swallowed hard but he managed a blank and innocent look. "I know maybe two-three Joes. Can't see this'n's face."

Bob backed to the dead man and turned his head so Hochner could look directly into the slack face. Once more, the rancher's throat spasmodically moved. "That ain't no Joe I know."

Bob sought to expose the lie with a bluff. "He said you were to meet him."

"Me? How could he say that when we ain't never seen one another? He pulled a whingy on you, Sheriff."

Bob strode to Hochner and looked at him with steady challenge. "Did he?"

"Well, seeing as he can't talk, you gotta take my word for it. What'd he do you had to shoot him?"

Hochner's eyes locked with Bob's in a challenge of his own. Bob recognized stalemate but he tried another attack. "What brings you this far from your spread?"

Hochner pointed across the valley. "Heard a man up that way near the Rim had some culls to sell. Turned out was wrong. So I'm riding home."

"Who was the gent?"

"Sam Blalock — Box B over in the next county." Hochner eased back in his saddle. "What's wrong about that? And I still don't know what *that* one did."

Despite what Bob had overheard beneath the man's own window, he had no witnesses to the plot he had overheard. Hochner had only to stick to his present story in court. If Joe could have been brought in alive, it would have been different. Still, a great deal had been gained. Through Hochner, Bob knew, he had a direct trail to the Brain. "All right, so you're white as any woolly lamb."

"But him — Joe?"

"You'll find out back in town — if that's where you're heading."

Hochner's gaze flicked to the saddle bags. Cupidity flashed for a second, vanished. "Figured to. Maybe you and —"

Bob's hand almost brushed his Colt. "I don't like company on a job. You'll head in alone. But first, drop your gun belt and rifle."

"Now listen here! You can't do —"

Hochner swallowed his words when he looked directly into the black, steady bore of a Colt. Bob said, "Just do as I say. You can get 'em at my office back in town."

Hochner slowly unbuckled his gun belt, keeping his hands well away from his holster. It thudded to the ground. A moment later, the rifle dropped in the coarse sand. Bob made a motion with his Colt toward the valley.

"Go that way. Might be the long way around but you could get killed trailing me in the canyon. Move out and keep going. I'll be watching."

Hochner's beefy face suffused. "You ain't going to get away with this, lawdog. Depend on it."

"Hope I can — and bring your friends. I want them all in jail. Now . . . *vamoose!*"

Hochner turned his horse back down the slope in the direction Bob had indicated. Bob watched him for long moments, then gathered up gun belt and rifle. Hochner looked back but Bob stood tall, legs slightly spread, and Hochner straightened after shaking his fist and rode on.

When Hochner had become no more than a moving black shape, Bob turned to the horses. He tied Hochner's weapons to Joe's horse, mounted his own and started the grim journey back through the canyon. The long and lonely desert would be safe now with Hochner disarmed and miles away.

Night caught him far from Singara. He stopped only long enough to build a small fire and to let the horses rest. As he cooked and ate, he kept his eyes and ears attuned to the gathering darkness. Hochner could not yet have reached his ranch but that did not preclude a chance encounter with others of the outlaw band.

His scant meal finished, Bob remounted and pushed on. He could no longer see the faint traces of the old road but he gave his horse its head. The animal would be as eager as he to get home and would go in a direct beeline.

In the darkest hours of early morning, he came on the Singara road and with a small sigh of relief turned into it. Hochner's ranch was not far away and the man might have reached it by now. If so, there might be watchers along the remaining dark miles to Singara. Bob rode with senses alert and hand never far from his holster.

Dawn came as he threaded the rolling hills and within an hour he saw the scattering of adobes ahead that marked the beginning of Singara. His horse sensed the end of the journey and, despite weariness, picked up its pace.

Thin pencils of smoke from chimneys marked breakfast fires and the bright morning street stretched deserted before him. He passed half a dozen houses before a man jerked open a door, jumped out into the street and stared at the body dangling across the lead horse.

"Who's that, Sheriff?"

"Outlaw. Now, why not get back to your breakfast?"

Bob rode on as the man bolted for his neighbor's house. The crowd would swiftly grow, Bob knew, so he increased his speed, turned the corner into Main Street and headed to the Wells Fargo station. The big yard gate yawned wide and Bob rode in. Several men harnessing horses to a huge freight wagon turned and immediately stopped their work. Bob reined in, swung out of saddle. "Close the gate. There'll be a crowd directly. Where's Mort?"

Just then Jerris stepped out of the office building. He pulled up short, looking at Bob, the lead horse, and the body tied across it, then back to Bob. "What in the world! Where have you been? Who's that?"

"He's called Joe, that's all I know. Recognize him?"

The gate slowly thudded closed as Bob unlashed the body, catching its heavy weight and easing it to the ground. Jerris looked down at the man and up at Bob with a soundless whistle.

"Joe Meghan. Works at the livery stable now and then — but not often."

Bob lifted a dead hand and pointed to the twisted, stiff finger. "We were told about this, remember? He's the man who shot Blaine. So he helped hold up the stage."

Jerris could only stare, speech forgotten. Bob turned to the heavy saddle bags, talking over his shoulder. "What gold rider was waylaid?"

Jerris blurted, "How did you know? You weren't even in town when he came in late yesterday."

Bob opened one of the saddle bags and revealed the dull, yellow bars. "Here's his delivery. Better check it out since I'd guess Wells Fargo was to get it."

"For shipment to the Frisco mint," Jerris

snapped and bent to the sack. "And here we all wondered why the sheriff wasn't around when we needed him! How did you know?"

Bob indicated the office. "Better talk in there."

Jerris became aware of his men crowding about. He picked up the saddle bags, turned on his heel and started to the office. Bob checked him. "What about Meghan?"

Jerris ordered his men to take the body to the carpenter shop and, as they bent to the task, Bob heard, "Twice he's brought in a dead outlaw. First thing you know —"

Bob hurried into the office after Jerris. A glance out the window revealed a crowd in the street. The bookkeeper and a clerk had forgotten their work and Jerris gave a swift order. "One of you get Dick Rohlens and Tom Clayson. The other keep the door locked and that crowd out of here. Get word to Buzzard Mine its bullion is safe."

Bob slumped wearily in a chair in Mort's office as the man checked the bars of bullion. "It's all here, Bob. I don't know how you did it but —"

A knock on the door interrupted him. Jerris opened to Dick Rohlens at the same moment that Tom Clayson pushed through the crowd in the street and was admitted through the outer door. Jerris waved them into his private sanctum and closed the door. He indicated the gold bars stacked on his desk.

"There's Buzzard's shipment. Bob brought it in along with Joe Meghan — dead."

Bob told what had happened, from his eavesdropping at Hochner's to the delivery of the gold. When he ended, Rohlens shook his head, "Meghan an outlaw and a killer! I'd never believe it. Not four days ago he curried my horse."

Clayson shoved his hands deep in his pockets as he walked grim-faced to the window and back again. "Well, now we know. And a lot of good it will do — unless Joe said something to Bob."

"Not a word. He saw my badge and went for his gun. He was dead when he hit the ground. It was that quick."

Clayson grunted, then his eyes narrowed. "But Hochner — now there's a man I never liked but I never figured him as outlaw. What about him, Bob?"

"Nothing — yet. What could I tell a judge and jury but what I'd heard? And no one with me to back it! He went to meet Joe to take over the gold, I know that. But . . . what proof other than what I heard and what I suspicion? A smart lawyer would make that damn clear."

"That's a hell of a thing!" Jerris snapped.

"Can't be helped. But I figure to keep a close watch on Hochner's spread. That is, soon as I can get some rest. Been up all night and rode all of yesterday."

Jerris looked around at his companions. "That gold could be almost anywhere in the wrong hands if it hadn't been for Bob. I'm thanking him personal, as well as for Wells Fargo."

"And for the town!" Rohlens burst out. "First thing you know, we won't have any more outlaws around here."

Bob pulled himself out of the chair. "I hope so. But there's a long way to go."

The bookkeeper pushed his head in the door. "Miss Madge is here, Mr. Jerris."

Madge Jerris fairly flew into the room, face alight. "I heard, Daddy! It's all over town!"

She turned to Bob, face aglow. "You went right out and faced those awful bandits — all alone!"

"Well, not quite —"

Clayson chuckled, nudged Rohlens and Jerris. "I think we're three too many in here."

Jerris hesitated but left with the others,

closing the door behind him. Madge stood close, looking at Bob with something so akin to adoration that Bob felt uncomfortable. "I just had luck — caught onto something and it all sort of fell into my hands."

"Nonsense, Bob James!" Her eyes lowered and she spoke with a note of uncertainty. "We've had our doubts . . . you know what I mean. But now — the way you've come in with an outlaw who tried to kill you . . . and the stolen gold!"

"Like I said —"

The light touch of her fingers against his cheek cut him short. She smiled tenderly. "So brave! and yet such a child! I can almost forgive . . . well, no mind now. It's over and the whole town knows how brave you are."

She suddenly leaned forward and her soft lips brushed against his cheek. She stepped back, flushed, but her eyes searching his a moment before she rushed from the room.

He stood rooted, elated and confused. He sensed that Madge had offered herself in her oblique words and she had also hinted that she now understood Verda Richards, and could afford to because a phase had ended. Bob tried to clarify Madge's almost deliberate vagueness.

Mort Jerris stepped back in the office. He looked sharply at Bob, then smiled and said,

"You'll be dog tired, Bob. Get home and have some rest. I hope you sleep better knowing how much I appreciate what you've done. Maybe Madge let you know how we all feel."

Bob's neck grew warm. "You make too much of a job, that's all."

It took some time to work his way through the crowd that demanded an account of the recovery of the gold. But at last he broke free and rode to his house. In half an hour he slept soundly. He awakened just after noon, had something to eat and made a round of the town. All seemed peaceful except for the continuing excitement of the morning. Everyone praised him and he found no refuge, even in El Ranchero where the banker and the miner, whose bullion had been recovered, wanted to ply him with drink. Two ranchers came in and the ritual threatened to be repeated, Clayson adding his own offer.

Bob finally escaped and started down the street, answering hails from doorways, strollers and riders. He was stopped by town matrons, the last time near the hotel. He was glad to break away from fulsome praise and escape into the lobby.

Obed stood just within the doorway and Mrs. Willets held station behind the counter.

They looked at him with strained, tentative smiles and Obed cleared his throat. "I reckon, Sheriff, we'd like to shake hands. We heard about what you did and if there's anything we can do for you . . ."

Mrs. Willets nodded stiff agreement. Bob accepted the proffered hands, then looked toward the stairs. "Matter of fact, you could tell Mrs. Richards I'd appreciate her coming down for a talk on the porch."

Mrs. Willets drew up, then recalled the peace offer and said dryly, "She went out some time ago."

He left the hotel, escaping a strained situation, and returned to his office. There was little to hold him and the day drew to a close. He soon walked across the field toward his house. He had taken but a few steps when he saw smoke rising from the chimney. He stopped in surprise.

Then he hurried to the rear door and stepped into the kitchen. Verda turned from the stove. She slowly rubbed hands along her apron as she looked uncertainly at him. "I figured you'd be home about this time — and hungry."

"Verda — you don't have to do this."

"I reckon so." She turned to the stove and spoke over her shoulder. "Wash up and set. It'll soon be ready."

He dropped his hat on a chair, suddenly wanting to put his hands on her shoulders, turn her about and kiss her. But some subtle thing in her stance checked him. He studied the burnished copper cascade of her hair and his gaze lingered a moment on her smooth, tanned arm working a spoon in a big pot.

"I . . . thanks, Verda. I'd sort of hoped for something like this."

"Wash up," she said without turning.

When he came back, she filled their plates with stew and coffee steamed from mugs. She gave him an underbrow look with sea-green eyes and made a small gesture to the table. "I cooked for me, too."

He laughed and took a step toward her but she turned to the table saying, "Better eat before it chills off."

He frowned, then sat down. It was still bright in the kitchen this time of the late afternoon. He ate the savory food, watching her. He told her about Hochner, his friends, Joe, and the recovered gold bullion. She nodded now and then. Twice she looked up, face alight. Then her lips moved in a puzzling expression and she gave full attention to her plate.

She arose when Bob finished the stew and brought dried apple pie with an apologetic,

"Sort of figured you'd like it."

As she placed the plate before him, Bob caught her hand. She started back and then surrendered to his grasp and steadily met his gaze. He said with sudden huskiness, "Verda, there's something I didn't tell you and —"

"Something I ain't told you yet. I'm leaving town."

XVII

He fell back, releasing her hand. She remained unmoving, braced for what he might say; and her hands slowly formed into tight fists. He recovered his voice. "Leaving! Why?"

"I figure now I can get by and not be charity forced on anyone."

"But when did you —"

"Oh, I just been waiting 'till you come back to tell you."

"You can't! I need you right here. You can help me."

"Seems like I've done anything but help you. I've heard what's said about you and me. It ain't true but that's no mind when folks really want to tear someone to pieces.. That's what all the old hens of Singara have been doing."

Bob started hot protest but knew that would be exactly the wrong thing. He controlled his voice. "Since this concerns me, we'd best talk it over."

"No need. My mind's made up."

"You're not being fair, Verda."

She started to protest, then slowly sank down in the chair across the table. Bob studied her a long moment and in that time relived his own discovery up in the desert canyon that he was in love with her. So now, seated across the table as though ready for flight, she could not leave him. Yet she would, on the instant, if he did not choose his words.

"I'm going to read clear, straight sign, Verda. First time you came into my office and said I had to do something about you, I got mad. Remember all the arguments I had why I couldn't do a thing and why you should go somewhere else?"

She didn't lift her head. He placed elbows on the table, leaning toward her. How beautiful and soft that bronze red hair! He checked the thought and tightly clasped his hands. "Then I saw how you could help me and I got the room in the hotel. I was right, wasn't I?"

"No," she muffled her reply.

"But I was! Why else did someone try to

kill you? It's because he didn't want you helping me, the sheriff."

"It's not that. Don't you understand? It's because the longer I stay around town, the more they talk about you. I know it."

"How do you know?"

She made a vague, palm-up gesture. "I just learned, that's all."

"Someone had to tell you."

She didn't reply. The minutes dragged and the silence built up tangible between them. She finally traced a tapering finger along the table edge but still did not speak.

"Clayson? . . . Tom Clayson?"

Though she still held her head down, he could see the silent move of her lips. He bored in. "It had to be him. He came to the hotel and —"

"Not him . . . first."

"Then, who?"

Again a silence and then she spoke with difficulty in a low voice. "First was that Mrs. Willets. She made me know what she thought about me. It wasn't much mind at first, scared and lonely as I was. She could think what she liked, but me — I had to have a place to live and something to eat. It was her first off."

Bob checked an angry retort. "And after her?"

"A lady . . . that's all."

"In the last day or two," he said flatly. "I'd bet my life on it. Who?"

"Just a lady. Friend of yours."

He blinked at that surprising statement. He recaptured her hand. She tried to jerk away but he held her firmly and forced her eyes up to meet his. "Verda, you can't let this go unsaid, even if you go."

"I promised —"

"What about me?"

She gently withdrew her hand. "It was . . . Madge Jerris."

"Madge!"

"She came to visit Mrs. Willets and I happened to be sitting alone on the porch. She came up and said who she was. She said the whole town knew all about me. She asked what I thought about you."

Verda walked to the open kitchen door. She stood with her back to Bob, arms crossed, hands grasping each elbow. He could see but part of her profile, the high bone and planed cheek, a twisted corner of her mouth.

"I told her I'd come to appreciate you as a good man — and no more. I made that plain as plain. She told me who her Paw is and that she knew why you'd put me up. But she said most folks said there was —

something between us. You'd come up to my room, she heard, and stayed there . . . saying it was law business."

"What did she know! What business — !"

Verda turned swiftly, face drawn but still holding herself close. "Ain't you seen? She likes you. More'n that. I could tell the minute she started talking. But no matter. She's right."

"She's dead wrong!"

He started to rise but her imperative gesture dropped him back in the chair. "No, you're wrong. Mr. Clayson — he come up as Miss Jerris and me talked. She asked him wasn't she right. She kept jaw-tugging at him and finally he gave in and said it was true."

She looked blindly out the open door. "It all tied in — what she said, and him. There's Mrs. Willets. There's a dozen times I've seen the town ladies cross to the other side of the street when they saw me coming. It's true."

For the first time he had a vivid picture of what must have been happening to her. He realized how cruel one woman could be to another. And the whole town! He said humbly, "I didn't know. I just didn't."

He rose and the small sound brought her around again. Her head lifted and her chin firmed. "So I'm leaving. The morning stage. Mr. Clayson — he gave me money with Miss Jerris right there. A loan, he said, and she said it was right for me to take it, seeing that the talk about you would die out."

His voice crackled the air. "You can't!"

"I am. I oughtn't to have come this afternoon. But I figured to do some last thing for you. I didn't mean to tell you."

He lunged across the room and grasped her arms before she could avoid him. "Verda! You can't! Listen, do you know what happened to me yesterday up in the Notch? It come to me while I was waiting for this Joe."

She tried to free herself. "No, Bob. No!"

"You — that's what come to me. It ain't because of how you can help me I want you to stay. It's because of me. I love you and —"

She wrenched free, turned blindly to flee but he held her by a shoulder and whirled her about. She buried her face in her hands.

"It's wrong . . . all wrong! Here you're sheriff and what am I? Outlaw's widow and drifter. I'm not right for you — not at all. You'll lose your job here and —"

He pulled her to him and she sobbed in his arms. He said softly, "Verda . . . Honey . . ."

She pushed away. When he tried to hold her, she beat at his chest. Tears streamed down her face and her lips moved in an agony of indecision. "I made up my mind. Clean and straight. I have to leave."

He held her. "Tomorrow? . . . Why? . . . You know how I feel . . . I never told you before. You got to think of me."

"I've thought!" she wailed.

"*Before* I told you I need you . . . me! You got to think some more."

She slowly straightened and he sensed a surrender. But when his fingers lightened on her arms, she shook her head and stiffened. "Just let me think. Like you said, I didn't know. But even so, it just ain't right."

"Think on it. Think on it hard."

She smiled wanly. "I reckon I'd better get back to the hotel."

"But you won't leave town before telling me?"

"Nnno. I promise."

So he let her go and stood watching her walk slowly away into the dusk. Then he turned back into the now darkening kitchen with a worried sigh. His thoughts lifted. She knew he loved her and that worked for him. But he could not quite hold to that new assurance. He grew restless and finally buckled on gun belt and left the house.

It was twilight, early for his first regular round, but he felt sheer bodily movement might bring some order out of his chaotic thoughts. He checked his office, then strolled toward the stores and saloons. Men spoke, and he sensed a new respect in their voices. He replied with a short but polite word. He forced himself not to look at the hotel as he passed and held his mind to the question of the bullion robbery.

He entered the stage station and found Jerris about to leave. "Just in time to have a drink with me, Bob. I reckon I owe you a million about now."

"One will do."

He waited as Jerris checked the lock on the big yard gate, tested the office door again and then they strolled slowly toward El Ranchero. Bob voiced the question that had been nagging at him.

"How you reckon the outlaws knew exactly where to hit that gold rider?"

"Beats me. Hazleton knew the route. All I knew was the time he'd ride in with the bullion. I never talked and I'm sure Hazleton didn't either."

"Then someone else did — to somebody."

"Just Hazleton and me knew," Jerris repeated firmly. "So how could anyone talk?"

They came to the saloon and Bob let the matter drop. The evening crowd had already gathered, merchants and ranchers. Mason talked to Hazleton at a far table, but broke off when he saw Bob and Jerris and waved them over.

Hazleton grabbed Bob's hand in a thankful grip. "You worked fast on this one, Sheriff. I'll not be forgetting it. The drinks are on me."

"Now *I* promised him," Jerris said with a chuckle.

The friendly argument went on, Hazleton finally winning. Bob listened idly, thoughts picking at the riddle as his gaze idly moved about the room. Clayson was not in sight. Bob wondered what he could say to the man after what Verda had told.

Hazleton's voice cut in on Bob's wandering thoughts. ". . . sure planned slick. My rider said he'd dropped into an arroyo to keep out of sight and there they were! One on each rim of the arroyo just above him, and guns lined right on his brisket. He said one of 'em squeezed off a shot to bring him to a halt."

Bob asked, "Where did this happen?"

Hazleton described the place and Bob put it some twenty miles east of Hochner's. The two men had plenty of time to reach it and set their trap.

Hazleton continued. "They made him drop Colt and rifle and the bullion bags. One of the outlaws told my rider to head down the canyon and be damned if he didn't follow for several miles along the rim just to make sure he did. He left the other one back with the gold."

"Honor among thieves?" Mason demanded incredulously.

"Sounds like it. Never knew one cutthroat to trust another out of his sight. Well, my man tells me the outlaw who followed him suddenly wheeled around. That was the last seen of him."

"Masked?" Bob asked.

"Bandannas. Both of 'em."

"Did your rider go back to where he was held up?"

"He figured they'd be gone and the gold, too. So he come right into Singara, looking for you. You were gone, so he reported to Mort."

"And I sent word to the mine."

"Then you don't know if Joe Meghan was one of 'em?" Bob asked.

"My rider looked at Joe's body but couldn't decide. What jiggers me is how you knew where to pick up the gold and this Meghan. You weren't even in town when my rider barged in with the news."

"I had a lead — and a hunch."

"But what was he doing up at the Notch?"

Bob exchanged a covert, warning look with Jerris and said, "Up to no good — what with the stolen bullion. I was lucky to get him."

"Lucky, hell! There's a lot you're not telling."

"Lawman's privilege," Bob grinned. "This round's on me and then I'd better get on the job."

The conversation turned general. Bob listened idly but studied Jerris and Hazleton, the old riddle returning. From a corner of his eye he saw Clayson emerge from his office and check with the bartender. Bob excused himself, pushed away from the table. He had a tight hold on resentment by the time he reached the bar and Clayson saw him.

"Well, Bob! You're the big man in town!"

"So they tell me but I don't feel like it. Had a talk with Verda Richards."

Clayson looked embarrassed. "So did I. She's told you? . . . Figures. How about my office?"

He entered the office behind Bob and closed the door. He met Bob's hard, questioning eyes. He shoved his hands deep in his pockets and moved to his desk.

"First, Bob, let me say I didn't go to the hotel to see the redhead. That was just some bad joshing."

"But you did go to her?"

"Yes. Madge Jerris and I met on the street and that young lady wanted to talk about you. Maybe you know it, maybe not, but she has an eye for you."

Bob flushed and Clayson said dryly, "I see you know. Well, that cuts out some explaining. You understand why she thinks Verda is doing you and your job no good. All that whispering. I agreed with her."

"Everyone wants to take care of me!" Bob snapped.

"That's right, we do. You're a good man, a good sheriff, and we like it that way. Anyhow, Madge and I agreed that Verda Richards might not be as bad as the gossip makes out. Madge would talk to her, woman to woman and let her know what Verda was doing to you. Then I'd come along and if she'd seen the point —"

"You gave her money."

"I *loaned* her money. Bob, I'll say no matter what she first had in mind, right now she wants things right for you. She understood what Madge had said and what I had to say. So, she's leaving — and it's all to the good."

"Is it?" Bob stepped close, fists doubled, and Clayson for the first time showed a touch of fear. Bob said, "I ought to beat the hell out of you. Only thing stops me is that you think you're really doing right."

"Believe me —"

"No, you believe me! Let Verda and me decide our own lives. The next time you stick an oar in, I'll just forget we were ever friends. You can depend on it."

He took a deep breath, glaring at Clayson. Then he turned on his heel and strode out of the office, leaving the door open behind him.

XVIII

Bob had hoped that Verda would make some sign but he did not have a glimpse of her. He tried to find where the outlaws could have learned about the gold rider and felt certain the key to the secret lay with either Hazleton, Jerris or both. So he caught Jerris in his office and asked a question that made the man stare in surprise.

"Of course, I was in town all that day! I was expecting the bullion, remember? As to what I did — I worked here, went home to dinner at noon, came back here — no, first to Dick Rohlens' store for canvas patching. Then here."

"Had a drink, maybe?"

"Yes, with Dick at El Ranchero and again, but alone, before I went home that night. What has this to do with the robbery?"

"Maybe nothing. No one trailed behind you, maybe?"

"No."

Bob sighed. "Well, that idea's out. Never did think much of it, anyhow."

He left the office and a puzzled man. But he knew Jerris' movements for the whole day. Bob looked speculatively at El Ranchero. After last night, Clayson might be mad, but Bob needed him. He glanced at the mid-morning sun and decided to allow a few hours more to soothe Clayson's possibly ruffled temper.

He turned to leave the station but halted in mid-stride as a rider turned the far corner off the Prescott road. Hochner's bulk could not be mistaken, even though the man's head was lowered against the hot morning sun. Bob took four or five quick strides into the station yard. He could now look back through the gate onto the street and, at this angle, see El Ranchero.

Hochner appeared in the street. He glared

angrily and defiantly about, gaze sweeping by the gate without seeing Bob half concealed within. Hochner looked at El Ranchero, reined in and sat a moment in the middle of the street. He turned the horse toward the saloon rack and dismounted.

His mount tied, Hochner surveyed El Ranchero's facade, taking in every detail. He looked down the street in each direction, his expression a defiant, angry hope that someone saw him. He deliberately spat on the first step of the saloon and then mounted to the porch and went in.

Bob moved into the street. What lay behind Hochner's angry and defiant move? Bob shot a glance at the man's horse, at El Ranchero, and then he crossed the street. He had just reached the rack when Hochner came storming out of the saloon. Clayson appeared behind him and Bob saw the small derringer in his hand. Neither man noticed Bob. Hochner shook his fist. "Not good enough for your fine friends, eh?"

"That's right," Clayson said. "I tolerated you a while. But we don't like dirty clothes or talk. If you come in again, I'll pull a gun on you if the sheriff doesn't first."

"And you'll have the gun shoved —"

"Trouble?" Bob asked and both men jerked about.

"No trouble, Bob."

"But there's gonna be!" Hochner growled. "I come in to get my rifle and Colt you stole from me, lawdog."

"I took 'em to keep you out of trouble."

Hochner said a scorching word of disbelief, jerked a thumb toward Clayson. "You're as all-fired uppity as this'n and the rest of the town. A man works hard for a living ain't worth treating human, is he? Not the way you see it."

"Come to the office. You'll have your guns."

Bob strode away. He heard Hochner's mumbled curses and then the sounds of the man's horse pulling up alongside. Bob strode on. Hochner glared at him and cursed again. Bob made Hochner wait outside while he went into the office and returned with the weapons.

He gave rifle scabbard and gun belt each a low pitch and Hochner grabbed them. Bob then threw two boxes, tightly tied with thin cord. "No shells in rifle or Colt and none in your belt loops. Keep those boxes tied until you get out of town or you'll land in jail."

"Riding high, ain't you!"

"Riding law," Bob corrected and indicated the way out of town. Hochner rode off with aggravating slowness. Bob gave him a long lead and then strode after him. Hochner rode to the Prescott road, turned north toward his ranch and disappeared. Bob halted then.

Clayson said from El Ranchero porch, "Thanks, Bob. But I had him on the run."

The man's anger had cooled since last night. Clayson beckoned Bob inside. Bob refused a drink but asked about Jerris.

"No, he didn't talk about the gold shipment — not that I heard. He and Dick Rohlens came in and Jerris worried about where you'd ridden off to. Dick told him he was just jumpy."

"Say why?"

"No, but *now* I know why — the gold rider."

"Hazleton?"

"Never talks about his business."

Bob thanked him and Clayson asked, "No hard feelings about me and Madge?"

"None — and won't be unless —"

"I stick my nose in again? No chance! Anyhow, I see she's not left yet."

"No."

Bob left the saloon, wondering what his next move should be. It still had to be Jerris or Hazleton talking. His mind suddenly clicked and he turned to frown back at the saloon. Since Verda hadn't put in an appearance all night or morning, how did Clayson know she stayed on? He looked across at the station and realized Clayson had only to watch departing stages.

He walked to Rohlens' store. The mayor worked in his office. "Mort was fretting all that day," he confirmed. "Told me he wanted you around and why. That gold rider was expected."

So Jerris *had* spoken to someone! Rohlens went on. "I calmed him down with a drink at El Ranchero and Tom helped get him out of his worries."

"Did Jerris tell Tom about the rider?"

"No."

"Did Hazleton?"

"He wasn't in town until late that night when Mort sent word about the robbery."

Bob worked that over, admitting it left him almost where he had started. He tipped his hat back from his forehead with a defeated sigh. "Well, anyhow it's over and one less outlaw."

"Amen to that!"

"Dick, I know Mort, the banker and the mines have to keep shipments a secret. But maybe the law — me — ought to know about them. I'd be chasing blind trails and the missing bullion out in the desert right now if it wasn't for my luck."

"I'd go for telling you. Mort left me all worried that day. I talked to Tom about it, him being a commissioner. But he didn't like the idea. Said one more knowing a secret makes it less of a secret."

"You and Tom talked about the gold rider?"

"He's county commissioner so I felt free to talk to him about Mort's problem. He'd not say I'd talked and he ain't. Most times all us city and county officers know what's going on. We work together. We don't let on to others we do it — but we do."

"Did all of you know about the money shipment due on that robbed stage?"

"No one knew I knew but Mort and Tom. From now on you'll be told things, seeing you're lawman. I guess we've been waiting to see how you work out before we really brought you in. But no point in keeping you out now. I'll tell Tom and Mort how it's going to be with you from now on."

"I sure wish I'd known how it was before this," Bob said ruefully and stood up. "But thanks for bringing me in your club. I'll keep my lips as tight shut as the rest of you have."

Bob left the store and walked thoughtfully to his office. The dim outlines of an ugly answer began to form. He couldn't quite believe it but he was lawman enough to know that his own feelings and beliefs had to pass the acid test of facts.

He stepped into the office and stopped short. Verda waited for him. His heart gave a jump of delight until he registered her troubled eyes and set lips. She thrust a folded sheet of cheap writing paper at him.

"It was under my door when I came back from breakfast this morning."

He read words crudely printed with a soft lead pencil. *"Your kind of woman ain't wanted in Singara. Stay more than two days and you'll stay in Boothill forever. We decent people mean it. We'll be watching the stages. See you're on one before sundown your last day of grace."* It was signed, *"Decent People."*

He folded the paper, face stormy. She said, "It proves what Miss Jerris and Mr. Clayson told me. I'm leaving."

"And leaving me?"

"You belong here. You're something but I'm owlhooter's widow, hashslinger, and boarding house flunky."

"You're the most beautiful woman I ever saw. You're the woman who's going to marry me — right here in Singara."

"That letter says not."

"Verda, I can tell you 'Decent People'

didn't write that. I'd guess it was the Brain or someone close to him."

"What!"

"You're dangerous to them. They'd rather not kill a woman but we know they'll try. They're giving you this last chance to scare out."

"I will."

"If I ask you not to?" He hurried on as she stared. "You have two days, and that's all I need. I'll have you safe forever in that time. I can break up these owlhooters."

"But how do you know it's them?"

"I think 'Decent People' and the Brain are the same. The Brain wanted ugly tongues to whip you out of town. You can let it happen."

"What would you do?"

"Verda, make up your own mind. I'll bring no pressure on you."

She studied him. "I think you'd leave, too. All right, I'll stay the two days."

He smiled and pulled her to him. Her lips firmed and then softened under his and her arms tightened about his shoulders. Then she shoved him away. "You shouldn't have done that. It makes it harder to — decide."

She darted out the door.

Bob folded the threatening note and fitted another item into place. Lips pursed, he thought of Hochner at El Ranchero. Considered one way, it was only a dull-witted man's defiance. Bob looked down at the note. But . . . another way?

Half an hour later, he rode to the stage station and borrowed Hanlon from Jerris. He deputized the man, saying he needed gun-siding in a job he had to do. He accepted Jerris' opportune offer to a drink and they went to El Ranchero.

Nursing the drink, Bob told Jerris and Clayson he'd talked to Rohlens and agreed all of them should know of important plans around the town and county. "Like now, I'm staking out Hochner's place. The man's in this banditry up to his filthy neck and I intend to prove it — and then see him hanged for murder."

He answered their excited questions and Clayson finally said, "I don't know. But anyhow be careful, Bob. We don't want to lose a good lawman."

Bob nodded and walked out of the saloon.

Hanlon, now armed and mounted, waited for him. As they rode out of Singara, Bob outlined his plan. The miles steadily rolled by. Bob cut off the road, angling toward Hochner's ranch. At last only a low, sandy ridge hid it from their sight and Bob drew rein. He pointed to a thick clump of cacti and palo verde cresting the ridge. "We'll make stake-out there. Natural place for one."

Hanlon frowned. "Maybe. But I'd bet sure as hell *they'd* know of it."

"So do I, if I've guessed right. So let's give 'em something to find."

He dismounted and removed a blanket-roll from the back of his saddle, telling Hanlon to follow suit. Bob studied the slope of the ridge, picturing the adobe ranch beyond it, and then placed his roll a few feet below the ridge and the base of the palo verde. Hanlon put his nearby.

Bob nodded. "It looks only like blanket-rolls now. But at night they'll look like sleeping men." Bob grinned at the dawning understanding in Hanlon's face, saw a second clump of ocotillo some distance off. "We'll sleep turn about over there, just below the ridge. We can watch both the ranch and this spot."

"Hope we get the chance to sleep."

They staked out mounts and climbed to the ridge to watch the distant ranch. Bob judged the sun, the ranch and the excuse for a road that led to it. He placed his binoculars beside him. "I figure Hochner will have visitors — maybe soon, but most likely late this afternoon."

Hanlon studied road and ranch. "Looks like they ain't no one there. We could be out here a mighty long time."

"Don't bet on it. Riders'll come from Singara — and they'll be looking for us."

"Will they now? Just two of us. How many will there be of them?"

"No matter. We won't do any fighting. I want your eyes and ears to back up mine, if I've guessed right."

Hours later, Hanlon nudged Bob, who dozed lightly just below the ridge. Three men rode to the ranch from the north. Bob swung glasses on them. "Hochner, Jowett and a stranger. Looks like a hardcase."

The three men rode into the distant yard and turned their mounts into the corral. Hanlon took the glasses. "I've seen the third one. Chuckline drifter. Turns up at Howie's saloon in Singara now and then."

Down below, the three walked into the ranch house. Hanlon asked, "Reckon they know about us?"

"Not yet. There'll be more visitors."

He and Hanlon spelled one another as the long afternoon waned into twilight. No one appeared and Bob began to have doubts. But all the factors had fallen into place so neatly this morning! He reviewed his reasoning and arrived at the same answer — or needed to have a new set of brains. He set himself to the watch.

A lamp came on in the distant house. Full night descended. Hanlon, safe in the darkness, stood up and stretched. "Maybe they'll come tomorrow?"

"I figured them here by now."

"No telling what the other feller will do."

Bob considered, gnawing at his lower lip. The single light in the adobe glowed steadily, became almost hypnotic. It was at least half a minute before Bob realized it had blinked several times. The meaning struck him. Several men had passed before the window, entering or leaving the adobe.

"Hanlon, I think it's going to happen. Muzzle our horses."

The deputy made a small sound of surprise. Bob slipped down the slope with him. The horses snorted but finally stout ropes around their muzzles prevented a whinny. Bob led the way back toward the blanket-rolls, halting several yards out from the tangle of cacti and palo verde.

Silence — deep and long. Hanlon started to speak but Bob's fingers clamped on his arm, silencing him. Time dragged. Then Bob heard a soft sound ahead and to his left, in the direction of the ridge. Another sound came from some distance straight ahead, beyond the blanket-rolls beneath the palo verde.

Hanlon heard it, too, and both drew their guns, waiting, hardly breathing. Silence for a long interval and then a whispered curse not far ahead. Bob stiffened as he saw a vague shadow moving toward the blankets.

Without warning, gun flame lanced and its thunder merged with that of a second and third gun. A shout sounded and boots softly thudded, converging on the blanket-rolls. A gun flamed and thundered again, followed by a second.

Hochner's bellow sounded clearly. "That got 'em. Jowett, give us a light."

A match flared and then a lantern glowed, grew stronger, and steadied. Bob saw the shape of half a dozen men about the blankets. So three had ridden up after dark! The lantern swooped low and Bob saw Hochner touch a blanket-roll and curse. Just then the lantern moved and a face came clearly in the light.

Bob instantly touched Hanlon, hissed, "Back! Out of here! Now! You saw Tom Clayson?"

"Sure did."

"Come on, then!"

XIX

They cat-footed back to their horses, leaving the angry sounds behind them. They released the muzzle ropes and swung into saddle. Without hesitation, Bob turned his horse up the slope of the ridge and Hanlon, with a whispered curse of surprise, followed him. They topped the ridge and dropped down the far slope in deep darkness, Bob holding the horses to a slow walk to lessen sound. All sounds of the ambushers cut off completely as Bob made the bold maneuver of riding directly toward the ranch house.

Bob circled to keep from being silhouetted against the light from the window. Now his senses probed both toward the house and any sound of alarm behind him. The squat adobe's black shadow slowly turned to the right until Bob and Hanlon paralleled its blind, dark rear. Then Bob lined out directly east, still holding his horse to a walk. When the house and its single glowing window were far behind, they set spurs.

They raced across the dark desert well north of the ranch road. Time and again Bob looked back but the night shadows disclosed nothing. They came to the Prescott road but Bob cut directly across it.

Hanlon spurred up beside him and Bob

reined in. The deputy said in an awed voice, "You scared the pants off me heading directly for the house back there."

"They'd figure we'd run away from it. And that made it safest of all."

"You got steel wire instead of nerves, Sheriff. That's all I can say. How come we ain't riding directly to town?"

"They'll watch the road." Bob's voice tightened. "Now . . . you saw Hochner back there and Clayson with him? You can swear to it in court?"

"I can. But I just can't believe Mr. Clayson is one of that gang."

"I think they call him the Brain. I made a point of letting him know we'd be watching Hochner. Sure enough — he showed up. They'll try to gun us down and shut us up."

"Might take some doing."

"Particularly if we stay out of sight — even in town."

"Ain't you going to arrest 'em?"

"Not out here, what with all their guns. They'll make another move in Singara. So let's head for home — roundabout."

It was almost dawn, after making a miles-wide circle, when the two weary lawmen came into Singara, avoiding the main street. They put up their horses in a small stable behind Hanlon's house, then Bob led the way to the hotel.

The high, black building seemed to slumber. Bob became satisfied that Clayson and Hochner wasted time in futile desert search, so had not yet returned to Singara. But they would. They had to.

Bob touched Hanlon's arm and motioned him to follow. They swung up over the balustrade of the hotel porch and edged along it to the door. Bob peered in. The lobby stood empty, a lamp burning low on the counter. A partially open door behind the counter told where the night clerk slept.

Signaling caution, Bob led the way to the stairs, eased up them to the hall above. Hanlon moved silently and closely behind him. Bob slipped along the corridor to Verda's door and tapped lightly. He tapped again . . . and again. He had a sudden, cold feeling that she may have left town after all. He tapped a bit harder.

He heard a muffled voice beyond the panels, "Who is it?"

"Bob. You're all right, Verda?"

"How do I know it's Bob?"

"Who was the last man to kiss you?"

Instantly the bolt sounded, then the key in the lock, and the door swung back into a dark room. The dim hall light barely touched the gowned woman who held a gun leveled. Bob glimpsed the dark sheen of burnished red hair as Verda said, "It *is* you!"

He stepped inside, pulling Hanlon after him. Verda stepped back as Bob closed and bolted the door. He gave a low warning. "Don't strike a light. Is there an empty room close?"

"Why — next door, I think. No one's been in or out and there's not a sound. These walls are thin."

"Hanlon, see if you can get in that room."

Hanlon left but returned in another moment. "Not even locked, Sheriff."

"Verda, go in that room while Hanlon and me stay here. Whatever noise you hear or whatever happens, don't open the door. Keep it bolted and locked and gun in your hand."

"What's this all about?"

"I found the Brain and he knows it. He'll believe you had something to do with it. His gang's hunting the desert for Hanlon and me right now to shut us up pronto. He'll be sending men to shut you up."

"But — who is it?"

"Tom Clayson."

She stared as Bob gently turned her to the door. "They could be here any minute so no time for talk now. Into the other room."

She moved swiftly out the door. When Bob heard both bolt and lock click home, he moved back to the other room. He gave a last look at the distant stairs, then joined Hanlon, closing and locking the door behind him.

He groped his way to the window and raised the blind. Night still ruled and there was just enough light to vaguely reveal the bed, chair and dresser. He outlined his plan to Hanlon, finishing, "And remember, no gunplay unless we're forced into it. We want whoever comes in alive to face a court."

Bob sat on the chair and Hanlon dropped on the rumpled bed to wait. Silence held the building and the night outside, but it seemed tense and dangerous. Dawn could not be far away but there was no lessening of the night that Bob could discern.

Time passed. Bob moved restlessly. If he had guessed right, the outlaws would soon make their move. He became aware that the building next door, seen through the open window, had faintly emerged from shadows, its wall an uncertain, dark gray. Now he could see the room furniture more distinctly.

He heard a faint sound beyond the door. A second later it came again, a step. He and Hanlon silently took station on either side of the door. They held Colts with hammers dogged back. Bob sensed someone beyond the door, close-pressing, probably listening. He thought he heard a whisper.

Then metal made a light sound in the lock. Someone had inserted a key, obtained from the board in the lobby, and tested it. The lock clicked back with a sharp sound. Silence again. Those beyond the door held breath and waited to see if the sound had awakened their quarry.

Bob tensed. He heard the slow, slow turn of the knob and he set himself, muscles tightening as he pressed back against the wall. A paper-thin crack of yellow light appeared. It grew slowly into a narrow band as the door inched back and back. Bob, in the increasing light, threw a glance toward the bed. In throwing back the covers, Verda had bunched them and a first, hasty glance gave the impression of a sleeper.

The door opened wider and a man stepped in, a second at his heels. Bob glimpsed Hochner's beefy face, eyes drilling toward the bed. The second man was the chuckline drifter Hanlon had identified back in the desert. Both men held Colts. They took another step into the room and Hochner pointed to a chair where Verda's cotton slip lay crumpled.

Without warning, Hochner's gun lined on the apparent body in the bed. It roared and flamed and a second shot thundered an instant later. Both men wheeled to flee but saw Bob and Hanlon at the same instant. The drifter reacted as automatically as a striking snake. His Colt came up but Hanlon's slug caught him in the chest, spinning him back over the foot of the bed. Hochner saw Bob's gun muzzle lined on him. He dropped his gun, hoarse voice croaking a strained, "No!"

"Turn around," Bob ordered.

He patted the man's clothing for hidden knife or derringer. Out in the hall, doors slammed open and men called excited questions. Verda, obeying orders, made no appearance. Bob indicated Hochner to Hanlon. "Keep this snake covered."

He stepped out in the hall, body blocking view of the room behind him. Men in underwear and nightshirts stood in four or five doorways. One held a gun but blinked sheepishly when he saw Bob's star. Bob holstered his gun. "Get back to your rooms, gents. Had a little trouble but it's all over now."

"That's the lady's room," one man stammered.

"Was. She moved. Like I said, it's all over."

Willets and his wife popped heads up out of the stairwell. The woman's eyes rounded and she caught her voice. It came out in a frightened, accusing screech. "Murder! In her room! I knew that woman would lead to trouble."

Bob thundered, "Mrs. Richards is not in the room. Verda, show yourself."

Verda's door opened. She looked at Bob, her strained eyes and face revealing her fear for him and her relief. The men suddenly realized their varied states of undress. As though on signal, they scrambled back into their rooms and the doors slammed. Bob ordered Willets to get the doctor. "We had to shoot a man here."

"Too late," Hanlon sang out. "He's dead."

"Bring Hochner out," Bob ordered and drew his Colt as Hochner stepped into the hallway, thick arms lifted, Hanlon just behind him with gun lined and hammer back.

Hochner stared in disbelief at Verda, growling, "So that's where they hid you!"

"Down the hall, Hochner," Bob snapped. "You're going to jail. Verda, stay in your room. I'll be back. Don't open to anyone but me."

Her breath expelled in a deep sigh of relief. She smiled and stepped back and the door closed. Bob heard key turn and bolt slide. Mrs. Willets sniffed and glared at Verda's door. "Things like this happening in a decent hotel!"

Bob ignored her, and marched Hochner out into the street, still dark although a faint streak of gray lighted the east. El Ranchero stood dark and silent; still it could conceal danger. The street was empty and Bob tried to guess Clayson's whereabouts.

He and Hanlon marched Hochner swiftly down the street. With a sigh of relief, Bob locked Hochner in a cell, then sent Hanlon to rouse Jerris, Rohlens and Aronson. "Tell them to get back here without being seen and not to waste time. It's getting on day."

He set himself down to wait. The street gradually became gray with dawn. Aronson appeared first, darting up on the porch, hair disheveled and shirt twisted from hasty tucking into his trousers. He asked excitedly, "You've rounded 'em up?"

"No, but enough to start. Mort and Dick will soon be here. I'll line it out when they come."

"How about Tom? He ought to be here."

Bob smiled tightly. "We're not forgetting Tom. Depend on it."

A few moments later Rohlens arrived and Jerris hurried in almost immediately, Hanlon at his heels. Rohlens looked questioningly around, "Bob, what's up?"

"I've got someone back here I want you to see."

He led the small procession back into the cell corridor. Beyond the bars, Hochner sat hunched on a bunk. Rohlens grunted, "Hochner! What'd he do?"

"He and a partner just tried to murder Verda Richards. Him and another partner tried to murder me and Hanlon last night. He led the outlaws that robbed the stage and killed the drummer and wounded Blaine. I'm seeing he hangs for it. He gave the orders."

Hochner's heavy head jerked up. "I didn't kill no one!"

"Maybe you didn't pull the trigger, though you sure did last night and this morning. Curt, I'm rounding up every one of your friends. I'm charging 'em with every crime in the book from murder down. Want to bet they'll take full blame for bushwhacks? For killing and robbing lone travelers? For stage coach and gold rider holdups?"

Hochner sat immobile, bulging eyes reflecting fear as Bob continued. "For sending Sonora Richards to kill me before I could even take over the badge? That's what Mrs. Richards told me and —"

"She lied!"

"You're the one called the Brain," Bob threw the bluff. "Too bad you can't hang for every man you've ordered killed or that your men have murdered. But at least once you'll dance a jig on the end of a rope."

Hochner's hand half lifted to his throat and his eyes glazed as his lips writhed to the horrible picture Bob called up. His hand dropped.

"You got it wrong, Sheriff. I ain't the Brain. I honest to God ain't. I just took orders, like the rest of 'em. I passed 'em along, that's the only difference."

Bob felt a rising sense of triumph. The man was on the point of ending outlaw rule and fear in Singara.

XX

Hochner jumped to his feet and peered at each man through the cell bars. He moistened his lips with a touch of sly sanity through his fear. He grasped the bars with both hands.

"If I tell, what happens to me?"

Bob said, "No promises. But if you talk, the judge might figure you tried to help at the last, anyhow. But if you don't . . ."

Hochner saw the picture of himself on the

gallows. "All right, I'll take the chance. The Brain is Tom Clayson — and always was."

Aronson, Rohlens, and Jerris gasped and Bob added, "It was Clayson who tried to kill me and Hanlon last night."

"Not Tom!" Jerris protested as though he could change all that had happened. "I don't understand."

"Hochner can clear it up. Start talking."

The big man behind the bars looked in turn at each face as though seeking some means of escape. But he found none and he started talking. He spoke of events in Singara long before Bob had arrived, of early rustling, of murders of lonely miners before the big strikes were made and the companies moved in, of mean little crossroads stores and saloons where renegades happened to meet and, as often, murdered one another for freshly stolen loot.

Hochner went on, "Clayson ended it. He come to me and said all of us were fools. If we quit fighting one another, we'd all get rich."

Hochner and several others had been convinced and the basic organization was set up. Clayson, catering to merchants, miners, and ranch owners, to the banker and the Wells Fargo manager, was in a position to know of cattle drives, money shipments, payroll arrivals, gold rider routes and schedules.

Jerris cursed. "And we elected him to the city council and a county commissioner!"

Hochner nodded. "It got so we never missed on a job. But Tom made us pass up penny-ante things. Some of the boys didn't want Tom and some of 'em still went out on jobs of their own. They didn't live long. So we ended up running the whole thing."

Hochner was momentarily proud and complacent, then continued, "About that time, some of you figured Singara needed a lawman. Tom bucked it until he figured you'd get suspicious. So he gave in." He pointed to Bob. "Sonora was sent to take care of you. He missed — but you didn't. Then before we could make another move that damn redheaded woman of Sonora's run off and come here. We figured she knew as much as Sonora."

Bob turned to his friends. "And I went to *Clayson* to ask what to do about her!"

Jerris demanded of Hochner, "Did you lead the stage robbers?"

"No. I never led any of the jobs. I just picked the men for 'em and they'd do the work. They'd take the loot to a spot where someone else would meet 'em — like Joe met the men who held up the gold rider."

He glared at Bob, then shrugged. "I was to take it from Joe and bring it to Tom."

Bob said, "That's what didn't make sense to me for a while — why the men who pulled a job would give up the money."

Hochner chuckled heavily. "Because if your posse caught Joe or one of the boys who held up the stage, they'd have no stolen money on 'em. The strongbox was emptied, the money counted, then passed on. It came to El Ranchero. I rode in a week later, took the boys' share, and divvied it up at my place. Same would have happened with that gold bullion, except Joe got caught."

"Raw gold," Jerris demanded, "how would you hide that?"

"We done it several times before. It went to Phoenix in one of your freight wagons."

"Damn! I remember! Tom shipped cases of whiskey to a saloon he owns there. Said he had too much stock."

"A couple of bars of gold in each case under the bottles," Hochner said in wry triumph.

"I upset the game," Bob cut in.

Hochner nodded. "Killing Sonora first. Then getting too close to that redhead. Then you began to have ideas there was someone in town heading up all of us. That made Tom afraid of you. He tried to scare

Verda out of town, having a man shoot through her window. He tried to get you to send her away. Then he saw a chance to work on her through Madge Jerris."

Bob said nothing to reveal how nearly Clayson had succeeded. Hochner swiped a hand across his mouth. "Killing Joe and seeing me up in the Notch brought you too close, Sheriff. Last night Tom rode out with three men after dark. He said you were staking me out and this was the time to get rid of you. We missed. We fanned out, trying to keep you from getting back to town. Then Tom thought of Verda Richards. If you were found dead, no telling what she'd say to the wrong people. Me and Tex said we'd shut her up."

Bob sighed, "So that's it. Where's Clayson?"

"Out in the desert with the boys. Hunting for you."

Bob gave the others a signal and they trooped back into the office. The men looked stunned. Jerris finally said, "Bob, you were the only one with sense enough to see it. But Tom Clayson!"

Bob checked his Colt and looked out onto the street, almost full-day bright now. Hanlon's raised brow silently asked a question and Bob said, "Clayson will know it's gone wrong by now. The hotel will be a'buzz."

Hanlon sucked in his cheeks. "How you going to handle it?"

Rohlens objected, "But he's out in the desert. Hochner told us."

"Tom Clayson's not fool enough to chase shadows across the sand. He knows he's missed me. He'll figure he has been seen. He sent Hochner and Tex to kill Verda just in case he and his renegades caught up with me. But long before now, he'll know I'm safe in Singara."

"But, then . . . he'd head right out of the country!"

"With just the money he has in his pockets? No, he'll try to slip into El Ranchero. A saloon safe can hold a lot of stolen money, Dick. At least, I'm going to see if it does."

"We'll go with you."

"Thanks, but what do any of you know about handling an outlaw? No, Hanlon and me will take care of it."

He signaled Hanlon and the two men hurried out of the office and down the street. The town showed signs of coming alive to the new day. When the two men made the turn, they saw a crowd had gathered around the hotel and its porch. Bob studied the situation.

"I'm cutting to the rear of El Ranchero.

228

Could anyone want a better cover than that crowd in order to slip in and out again?"

Hanlon spat. "I'll stay out front until you show your face or there's trouble inside."

Bob hurried to the wide alleyway behind the long line of buildings. Near the hotel, he could faintly hear the excited voices from the other side of the building. The rear of El Ranchero came in sight, a thick, low adobe wall broken only by a door and a single window so dusty that no one could possibly see in or out.

Bob wondered if he had guessed wrong and that Clayson still searched the desert or had fled to some distant hiding place. He rejected the thought and, lifting his gun from its holster, raced to the door, watching for movement behind the dirty window.

He grasped the knob and slowly turned it, pulling his weight away from the door. He felt rather than heard a slight click and he pushed the door slowly open. A single step took him inside and another placed him against a wall out of the frame of the doorway. He stood listening. He was in a short hallway with two securely padlocked doors to either side. Ahead was another door, partially open.

Bob moved silently along the wall. When he reached the door, he could see a part of the big main room of El Ranchero. Clayson's office would be just along the wall against which his shoulder brushed, but he could not see the entrance.

He could hear a murmur of crowd voices now, the curious milling around the hotel. Then another sound came, loud within this silent building. Clayson appeared, hurried across the room to the front door, and boldly opened it, preparing to leave, knowing the crowd would pay him no attention.

Bob placed a hand on the door frame to swing it wide, jump inside the main room, and confront Clayson. Before he could move, a gun that could only be Hanlon's blasted out in the street, the thunder echoing in the big room. Bob stood stiff in surprise for a split second. Then he slammed the door back and lunged into the big main room.

He saw bright dawn light streaming through the open front door across the room. He had a glimpse of Clayson, saw flame spit and tongue from the gun in his hand, the slug directed out into the street. The ornate glass of the door shattered as an answering slug screamed into the room.

Clayson jumped back. Bob saw the bulging saddle bags he had thrown over his left shoulder. At that instant, Clayson saw Bob.

His eyes widened and the Colt he held swung around and up. Both guns roared in a symphony of thunder and flame. Muscle, flesh, bone, and form vanished in a giant's blow to Bob's right shoulder. He felt himself falling. Clayson vanished. Then the smooth, clean sawdust of the floor filled Bob's eyes, nose and mouth. Creation whirled dizzily and vanished as though sucked into a dark vacuum.

The world returned in the blink of an eye. But a different and strange place. Bob looked at a heavy desk and thick safe in a small room. He saw a window covered with heavy drapes. After a moment of clear vision, the room swam and he closed his eyes.

He opened them again to look up into Verda's strained, beautiful face, her sea-green eyes glowing like emeralds as her face lighted. Bronze hair framed soft, tanned skin and her lips formed words that slowly registered. "Oh, Bob! Thank God!"

Her hand touched his cheek, smoothed along the jaw. Something moved beyond her and Dick Rohlens came into focus. Bob identified Jerris and Hanlon. Doc Laren loomed over him, moved away with, "He's out of it. But don't push him."

Bob suddenly remembered Clayson, the open door, the blast of a Colt simultaneously with his own. He tried to find connection between that scene and this room. He remembered a sawdust floor swooping up to meet him. He looked up as Verda again appeared over him and he tried to form words through lips that seemed detached and unmanageable.

She smiled, shook her head. "Don't talk. You'll be all right. You're in the El Ranchero office. We'll take you home as soon as Doc gives the word."

His right shoulder, arm, and hand still felt numb and ghostly. Doc Laren appeared again, said, "Nicked bone and shocked nerve. It'll hurt like hell for a while but then be all right. Give it a month and you'll be able to handle a Colt again."

Rohlens moved up. "Sheriff, you've done a job. Clayson's dead and Hochner's in jail. It's damn surprising how many chuckline riders have taken off for the long trails yonderly."

Jerris edged Rohlens aside. "I sure apologize for not believing you, Bob. Clayson was delirious his last minutes but he talked just enough sense that we know he *was* the Brain. He had a lot of hardcases we never suspected working for him. You've broken up outlawry in Singara for years to come."

Bob tried to speak. "No . . . always out-

232

laws. Lawman never . . . rests."

"But no band of 'em," Jerris insisted. "Thanks to you."

Bob's eyes turned to Verda. "And thank . . . her, too."

Rohlens and Jerris turned and thanked her with no note of insincerity or withdrawal in their voices. Verda flushed, looked uncomfortable, and looked toward the door as though she'd like to flee. Bob groped for her hand. Her face lighted and, forgetting the men, she grasped it, leaning toward him. Bob looked at Rohlens, Hanlon and Jerris. "Figure some changes . . . Hanlon, now . . . a deputy?"

"Fine!" Jerris agreed

"But . . . something else. Your sheriff . . . might be a married man. That is, if she'll have him . . . and Singara still wants me to wear the star."

Verda's fingers tightened around Bob's in rigid surprise. Her eyes became misty sea-green and she seemed to hold back tears. Then her lips tried to form words. Suddenly she dropped beside the divan and leaned to him, lips seeking and finding his. "Oh, Bob! . . . I — of course, I want you! But —"

"Verda . . . no but's."

Doc said with mock severity, "All of you

sure keep my patient resting easy! How you reckon he'll be in any condition to move?"

Rohlens chuckled. "Doc, we want to make sure he keeps the star. Ain't that right, gents?"

The rest nodded emphatic approval. Doc growled, "Leave him alone until I get him home. He can't stay in a saloon office and do any healing." Doc grinned at Verda. "Except you. If you just hold his hands, you're better'n medicine."

The men grinned and started to move out, though Jerris hesitated. Bob heard Rohlens say as he went through the door, "Hanlon, you hold down the law office while Bob mends, hear me?"

At the door, Jerris turned, looked long at Bob and longer at Verda with an air of apology. "Got to say it, Ma'am. So excuse me. You got a good man. I only wish he could've been my son-in-law."

He smiled wistfully and walked out. Verda turned to Bob. Doc's gruff voice sounded behind her. "I'll make arrangements to move him. No point in me telling you not to kiss him. But you might sort of remember that shoulder of his."

The door closed behind him.

The employees of Thorndike Press hope you have enjoyed this Large Print book. All our Thorndike, Wheeler, and Kennebec Large Print titles are designed for easy reading, and all our books are made to last. Other Thorndike Press Large Print books are available at your library, through selected bookstores, or directly from us.

For information about titles, please call:
  (800) 223-1244

or visit our Web site at:
  http://gale.cengage.com/thorndike

To share your comments, please write:
  Publisher
  Thorndike Press
  10 Water St., Suite 310
  Waterville, ME 04901